Disclosure of the *Heart*

Mary Whitney

OMNIFIC PUBLISHING
LOS ANGELES

Omnific Publishing
1901 Avenue of the Stars, 2nd floor
Los Angeles, CA 90067
www.omnificpublishing.com

First Omnific eBook edition, November 2013
First Omnific trade paperback edition, November 2013

The characters and events in this book are fictitious.
Any similarity to real persons, living or dead,
is coincidental and not intended by the author.

Library of Congress Cataloguing-in-Publication Data

Whitney, Mary.
    Disclosure of the Heart / Mary Whitney – 1st ed.
    ISBN: 978-1-623420-97-0
    1. Contemporary Romance — Fiction. 2. First Love — Fiction.
    3. New Adult — Fiction. 4. Washington, DC — Fiction. I. Title

10 9 8 7 6 5 4 3 2 1

Cover Design by Micha Stone and Amy Brokaw
Interior Book Design by Coreen Montagna

Printed in the United States of America

To Mr. Cat, my dear writing companion.
This was his last book.

Chapter One

Nicki Johnson
Washington, DC
January 2009

The hardest lies to maintain are the ones you tell yourself. For me, one way or another, the truth always seeped through the cracks of my brain. It was the biggest day of my career, and my mind should have been on something important, something that might come up in the next hour — like the Middle East or domestic gas prices or health care. Instead, all I could think about was Dolly Parton. That song "Here You Come Again," which had haunted me for days, was at it once more, ringing through my head.

Trying to refocus on work, I glanced about the packed room as reporters chattered away while they found their seats. I avoided looking in the back left where I knew *he* was sitting. The assigned seats in the White House press briefing room were designed so the press secretaries would always know which news outlet they were talking to. I just happened to also be using the seating chart to avoid seeing my high school boyfriend.

"It's time," I heard Matt, my boss, whisper in my ear.

Nodding, I watched him take to the podium, and as he adjusted his microphone, the chaotic room became orderly at once. The inauguration might have been yesterday, but this was the first press conference in the White House—a momentous event for everyone in the room. The media were on their best and brightest behavior, waiting for the White House press secretary to speak.

"Good morning to you all. Welcome to our first official press briefing," Matt said in his booming voice. His belly, big from months of bad campaign food, shook as he chuckled. "I'm sure we'll soon get sick of seeing one another every day."

The room reverberated with laughter, and I attempted a genuine smile, but an observant person would've seen it was tense. If you had noticed, you'd have probably thought I was nervous about work. Not at all. Work didn't make me anxious. My job was easy for me—always had been. The guy who sat somewhere in the back, well, that was tough. He was best kept out of sight and out of mind.

After the crowd quieted, Matt said, "Before we get started, I want you to meet our team. First, I'd like to introduce you to our deputy press secretary, Nicole Johnson. If you were on the campaign trail with us, you know Nicole well."

I was blocked from view by a few of the male staffers, so Matt gestured toward us and said, "Nicole, get out from behind Jeff so you can say hello."

Placing all thoughts of Dolly Parton songs and ex-boyfriends out of my mind, I stepped around Jeff and the guys and gave the room a small wave. Matt offered me the podium, and I was in my element. With a confident smile, I said, "Hello, everyone. Being new in town, it's nice to see some familiar faces from the campaign. And I'm looking forward to getting to know those of you I haven't met yet."

"Thank you, Nicole," Matt said, showing me back to my space. He leaned in toward the microphone to crack his standard joke. "Unlike me, Nicole has all the answers. Just try to stump her."

I smiled and shook my head just like I always did, and Matt continued with the introductions of our staff. Afterward, the questions began with the press studiously taking notes as Matt recited policy positions we'd both repeated a thousand times. Yet everyone hearing the words that day knew they were different. This was no longer a presidential candidate's position on a critical issue. It was now the position of President James Logan's administration. The enormity of the moment struck me, and I had to remind myself, *Wow. I work for the president.*

As if he read my mind, my most dedicated staffer, Jeff, whispered in my ear, "Can you believe this is happening to us?"

With a smile, I said under my breath, "No." And he didn't know how much I meant it. There I was, part of a little moment of history, and Adam Kincaid—of all people—was in the room with me. How did *that* happen?

I shifted my eyes slightly to the left toward the back where I knew he was, but I was too short to really see him. All I caught was a glimpse of his rusty hair towering over the crowd. When I'd known him, it was longer, but it made sense it was short now—he wasn't in high school anymore. And neither was I.

Adam heard my introduction, and tall as he was, he must've seen me. I wondered what he thought. Did he still think I was pretty, even a little? Or did I look old? I was short with mousy brown hair; I certainly didn't look like the women I knew he dated.

My stomach lurched in a way I hadn't felt in forever, and the Dolly Parton song floated back to me. She sang about a man walking back into a woman's life, just to wreck it again.

My head snapped to attention. *No.* That wasn't going to happen to me—not this time.

I peeked again toward the back. The question wasn't *how* we'd gotten to the same place. You could easily trace that by our professions; it could've happened to anyone on our career paths. I'd just moved to DC because I was a communications staffer for a successful governor who'd become president, and Adam had already been here for a few years heading the BBC's Washington office.

The question was *why*. Why had he gone back to beat reporting and taken the job at the White House? Was it just because it was an exciting new presidency? Or did he care that I was there?

My heart sank with shame and guilt. I shouldn't have been thinking those things for many reasons, but I did. How could I not?

The inevitable moment came when Adam was called on for a question, yet I still wasn't ready for it. When Matt announced, "Adam," I flinched so hard that Jeff gave me a side eye. He clearly wanted to know why I'd have a physical reaction to a BBC reporter—it wasn't like an Al Jazeera reporter was about to speak. I ignored Jeff and played nonchalant. No matter how much I wanted to step forward and get a better look at Adam, I had to stay back. I hadn't gone out of my way to look at any other reporter, after all. Adam should be no different.

I took a deep breath as Adam's distinct English accent filled the room. "As a candidate last autumn, the president made lukewarm comments toward the relationship between the United Kingdom and America. Is the Logan administration going to mark a new era in the two countries' special relationship?"

His voice was deeper than I remembered it but still familiar. My hands clenched into fists so tight, I felt my nails cut into my palms, and my heart hung on his words. Had Adam meant anything by "special relationship"?

As Matt answered his question, saying the special relationship was as strong as ever and comments during a campaign had to be taken with a grain of salt, I realized I was a total idiot. Adam had asked the question any BBC reporter would ask at the start of a new American presidency. He was only quoting Churchill, not signaling anything to me. *Get a grip, Nicki.*

When Matt moved on to the Univision reporter, I forced my fists open and splayed my fingers, hoping to ease some of my tension. I turned to Jeff and found something relevant to say.

"Remind me to follow up with Univision," I whispered.

"Sure," he said. "Any international press? The BBC?"

"No." It came out a little curtly and much too quickly. I added in a nicer tone, "There's no reason to."

There really wasn't.

After the briefing was over, I remained in the front, knowing reporters would come to me. I wouldn't have to walk the room and bump into Adam. Of course, I'd soon have to talk to him. My job would require it, but it didn't have to be today.

Thankfully, the clock ticked away, and I let my eyes stray up to it even when I was in the middle of answering a question. Matt and I had a meeting at the top of the hour. He hated being late, so we'd have a quick exit.

With only a few minutes to get to the next meeting, I gave my final instructions to Jeff, waiting for Matt to tap me on the shoulder to signal our departure. After Jeff scurried off, behind me I overheard Matt say, "Welcome, Adam. I hear you're going to be with us for a while."

I gulped and looked around in desperation. There was no one to talk to. The only appropriate move would be for me to turn and follow my boss's lead in welcoming the new BBC reporter. That's what someone in my position would normally do. It was what *should* be done.

And it was my perfect opportunity to strike two birds with one stone. I could talk to Adam using Matt as a buffer, and I could also casually tell Matt that Adam and I knew each other outside of work. In the interest of full disclosure, Matt should know that I once had a personal relationship with a reporter covering the White House. I just hadn't said anything yet because it was never the right time. That's what I told myself. I didn't want to make a big deal of our acquaintance because it wasn't a big deal, right?

"Yes, thank you," I heard Adam answer. "I'm looking forward to it."

I expected Matt to say something else, but instead I felt him tap my shoulder and then walk toward the door. I was off the hook. I could leave and avoid Adam altogether.

Yet in the end, I couldn't simply walk away from Adam. I couldn't ignore the fact he was right behind me. After over fifteen years and an ocean between us, he was now only a few feet away.

Without an additional thought, I wheeled around to finally see him.

As much as I'd tried to get Adam out of my mind in the last few days, I had done some preparation to meet him again. I'd expected to see him handsome as ever and be charmed by his smile and speech. After all, he was a funny, great guy. I was supposed to say, *"Hello, how are you?"* and *"It's nice to see you again."*

Standing before me, he *was* handsome, his smile *was* charming, and he seemed genuinely happy to see me, but I couldn't return the smile. I couldn't say any of my practiced lines. Seeing him flooded my mind with memories I'd long ago chosen to forget.

They were bittersweet memories of him and, most startling, buried memories of my sister. The aftermath of Lauren's death was a part of me I'd only shared with him, no one else, no other friend and certainly no other man. Adam wasn't just an ex-boyfriend, because he really hadn't been a boyfriend in the first place. When we were together, he'd been my life, or at least a lifeline when I had needed it most. And then he'd broken my heart, and though he'd desperately tried, all the king's horses and all the king's men couldn't have put it back together again.

There in the middle of the White House, I locked eyes with him, and all the pain I'd known stabbed at me. I was seventeen again, with a scarred body and a shattered life.

One day a few years ago, I had watched as my cat approached a squirrel in my mom's backyard. The squirrel had been motionless, petrified by fright. Instinct told the animal that any movement would only make him more vulnerable. That was my reaction to seeing Adam; I said and did nothing. I stared at him with no expression, like he was stranger on the street.

"Nick—" he began to say with a broad smile before Matt spoke over my shoulder.

"Nicole, we need to move on."

Matt was my way out of this emotional disaster. Like a robot, I turned on my heel and followed him without looking back. Closing my eyes, I tried to find reality, but maybe it was reality that had already hit me.

I remembered my last conversation with Adam fifteen and a half years before. In a most vivid memory I didn't allow myself to think of often, the boy I'd once known spoke through his tears, *"I'm not saying goodbye. I love you too much to say that."*

The impossible had occurred. Adam was in my life again, even if it was only professionally. I couldn't deny our past. Warmth welled in my heart, and a joy inside reminded me, *It's Adam!*

I stopped for a moment and peered over my shoulder, still unsure how to act around him. I noticed he'd taken a step back and his brow had furrowed, just as it always had when I'd confused him. That made me smile, but a smile was all I could muster. I left without saying a word, more confused than he was.

Chapter Two

As Matt led us through the West Wing, I checked my phone, knowing all the messages waiting for me would shock my system back into work. The texts were usually the most important, so I scanned them first. I was surprised to see one from Lisa, my best friend from growing up in Texas and whom I'd been crashing with since I'd come to DC.

Why haven't you called me back???

I went to my received calls, and there were three from her. Normally, we didn't bother each other at work. She took her job as seriously as I took mine, and the clock on my phone warned I had no time to call her back. I quickly tapped out a reply.

Sorry. Busy. Can't talk right now. What's up?

Her response flashed almost immediately and caused me to stop in the middle of the hallway.

WTF? Why didn't you tell me ADAM KINCAID was in DC and WORKING WITH YOU?

I stared at the screen. Maybe it was because we'd been friends since sixth grade that we kept some things from each other. We didn't offer information, nor did we pry. Certain subjects were simply off limits. Why would we want to cause a friend unnecessary pain? Lauren was one of those subjects for me, as was Adam.

Yet, sometimes a topic had to be addressed. Adam being in DC was a major one that I'd avoided but known she would eventually find out. Either I'd be forced to tell her, or it would come up somehow. I just didn't expect it so soon. I tried to deflect her.

Sorry. And I don't actually work with him.

In only seconds, she called me out on my shit just like she had since we were kids.

Whatever. Why didn't you tell me?

She was onto me. I had to acknowledge I'd screwed up, because Lisa was not one to let something go. I gave her my one-word answer as to why I'd left her in the dark.

Denial.

And then came her reprimand.

You're crazy.

I snorted at that.

*Yeah, I am, but why are you watching
the news at work anyway?*

My distraction didn't really work.

*I wanted to show you off to my colleagues.
Geeky scientists think I know a celebrity.
I didn't expect to see HIM on the screen. We HAVE to talk.*

That was such an unsavory proposition that I got a bad taste in my mouth. Reluctantly, I replied.

Okay. Tonight.

After Lisa's rebuke, I decided I had to tell Matt that day. I wanted him to hear it from me before anyone else in case there was gossip. Who knew whom Adam had talked to or what he'd told them? Because it was the journalistically ethical thing to do, I guessed he'd said something to his bosses at the BBC. But what? Whatever it was, it hadn't been enough to stop him from covering the White House. So maybe this whole past-relationship thing actually wasn't so earth-shattering.

Regardless, I didn't have a moment alone with Matt until after seven that evening. By that time, his tie was loose and his jacket off, and he was always a little flippant when the workday slipped into the night. When you spoke to him, he'd make snarky comments and sneak glances at photos of his family lining his desk. He just wanted to get the hell out of there and home to his wife and kids. If you had an issue you wanted dealt with quickly, nighttime was always the right time.

I poked my head into his office. "Got a second before you leave?"

"Sure," he said, looking up from his laptop. He continued typing as he talked. "What do you need?"

"I've been meaning to tell you something." I leaned against the doorjamb and crossed my arms, hoping to signal that if I didn't sit down, it wasn't worth a real discussion.

"What's that?"

"Just that I knew Adam Kincaid in high school."

Smiling, Matt cocked his head and leaned back in his seat, giving his belly a wide berth from the desk. "Adam with the BBC? How did that happen? I thought you went to high school in Texas."

"I did."

"Was he an exchange student or something?"

"No. His dad is a geologist and worked for a year in Houston for an oil company."

"Wow, what a coincidence. Were you friends?"

It was the logical question, but I wanted to laugh. Adam wasn't my friend. We were never friends. If he'd been my friend, I would've stayed in touch with him over the years. But if I told Matt no, I'd lead him completely astray. I had to at least disclose there had been something romantic between Adam and me.

I shrugged. "We went out…a few times."

As soon as I said it, I kicked myself. I shouldn't have added "a few times." I'd just lied to my boss. Yet if I left it open, he could probe more. How could I tell him anything else? I never talked with anyone about Adam.

Matt placed his hands behind his head like he always did when he wanted to enjoy a juicy story. He snickered and asked, "So you kissed him?"

What a question. What *hadn't* I done with Adam? Hoping a joke would make everything feel less like a lie, I smiled and said, "Maybe."

That brought out Matt's big belly laugh. Thank God for sexual harassment laws because he didn't press me on the issue and instead moved on. "So did you keep in touch after he left?"

"No, but I've kept up with his sister, Sylvia." I took a deep breath, happy I was back in the land of the complete truth. "She lives in New York."

His tone became more serious. "I suppose I should ask if you plan on striking up something romantic with him again."

"Uh, no." My response was immediate and without forethought. I was pleased of that. Though I wasn't proud of the twinge of regret I felt after I'd said it.

"Just asking. You know it's my job to look out for that sort of thing," he said, looking at his watch. "I need to get going. Thanks for letting me know. I don't see it as a problem."

"Thanks. Have a good night."

"You, too."

I turned around, feeling like I'd gotten away with murder but happy for it all the same. Yet just as I took a few steps away, I heard him say, "Oh, Nicole."

"Yeah?" I asked, looking over my shoulder.

Matt wore his most devilish grin. "Have you told Juan Carlos?"

I froze at the thought, but somewhere I found a smile to fake for the moment. The best thing to do when you don't want to answer a question is change the subject. I rolled my eyes and said, "I gotta go. I need to catch my train."

But Matt knew me too well. As I walked away, I heard him laugh. "I didn't think so." A few seconds lapsed, and he called from his office, "You know what they say about jealous Latin men!"

As I made my way home on the Metro that night, my guilt became so heavy it was crippling. I wanted to curl up in a ball right on the floor of my train. How was I leaving Juan Carlos in the dark? He was my loving, wonderful boyfriend. He didn't deserve that, and yet I saw no way out. As bad as the conversation was going to be with Lisa, it was nothing compared to the talk I should have with Juan Carlos.

Walking up Connecticut Avenue, I dreaded every step toward Lisa's apartment. Though she was only in town for a year, working on a fellowship at the National Institutes of Health, she'd lucked out in the hunt for DC real estate. A molecular biologist off on a sabbatical at the Pasteur Institute in Paris had sublet his place for cheap.

When I walked into the living room, I saw Lisa sprawled on the sofa with a blanket as she talked on the phone. She waved hello, pointed at the phone, and then looked to the ceiling as if that might offer some help. She had to be talking with Elliot, her on-again, off-again boyfriend back in Houston. Like Lisa, he was an MD/PhD, so he was smart enough for her, but unlike her, he was a total dork. She swore he was the last white guy she was ever dating.

While she was occupied, I fled to my room, changed into yoga pants, then wandered into the kitchen for a glass of wine to accompany the leftover pizza in the fridge. I took my dinner to the dining room along with my iPad to catch up on my dirty little addiction to celebrity gossip.

After a few minutes, Lisa joined me with the wine bottle in hand. "Hey. How are you?" she asked.

"Okay," I mumbled.

"Ha!" she laughed and topped off my glass. "You need another drink."

"I do." I sipped some wine and said, "I bet you do, too, after talking with Elliott. What's your status now?"

"Limbo." She pulled out two chairs, sat in one, and put her feet up on the other. "Which is fine while I'm away."

"Limbo has its benefits. Is he coming to visit at all?"

"I told him I don't have time for guests right now — at least while you're living here." She waited a moment and added, "For however long that is."

I got the hint. Swirling the wine in my glass, I said, "Only for a bit."

"Don't get me wrong. I'd love for you to stay here." She smiled. "I've missed you. It's been years since we spent this much time together."

"I feel the same way." I raised my glass. "To lifelong friends."

"To best friends." She clinked her glass to mine, and we both took drinks. Afterward, she gave me one of her signature knowing looks. "And since we're best friends, why — "

"I know. I know," I cried out in exasperation with myself. "I should've told you. I just didn't want to talk about it."

"Well, that's nothing new."

"I'm consistent." I laughed.

"When it comes to Adam, yes, you are." She shook her head. "Have you told *anyone?* Shouldn't your boss know?"

"Of course I told Matt," I said with proud indignation. She didn't need to know that I'd only just told him a few hours before.

"What did you say?"

"Just that I'd dated Adam a few times in high school."

When you've known someone practically your whole life, there are times when verbal communication is completely unnecessary. Lisa remained quiet and stone-faced, but her eyes said everything she was thinking. She thought I was crazy—a certifiable psycho-lady, Queen of Denial. She also had some knowledge—though not all—as to why I was so wiggy about Adam Kincaid.

For my sake, I'm sure, she apparently decided not to say everything she thought, but she still shifted in her seat, signaling she was uncomfortable with my lie. "Well…that's accurate…in a way."

"Give me a break. I'm not going to go into details, especially when it's irrelevant."

"*Is* it irrelevant?"

"Of course."

"Have you told Juan Carlos?"

"Not yet."

"Oh dear God," she groaned.

"I'm telling him tonight. I swear."

"Does he know anything about Adam?"

"I don't know…"

"What have you said?"

"Nothing, really."

"Nicki…"

"Please. I don't want to hear about Juan Carlos's exes. I'm sure he doesn't want to hear about mine." That was only partially true. We had spoken in vague generalities about our past love lives. It was a testament to how much I loved him that I'd actually told him about a guy in high school who'd cheated on me. I hadn't told him I'd been crazy about the guy, however, and I certainly hadn't said it was Adam. With a flick of my hand, I spoke like I was tossing the issue aside. "Besides, it was a long time ago."

"Bullshit."

"What?"

"You heard me. Bullshit." She leaned forward and placed both hands on the table to make her case. "If Juan Carlos started working with someone he'd once been in love with, you would want to know."

"Yes, but—"

"*Especially* if he'd never gotten over the girl."

My mouth dropped open both in shock and an attempt to find something to say in response. Though nothing came out, it was enough of a reaction for Lisa's expression to turn into a sad frown. "Oh, Nicki. I'm sorry. I don't want to be mean. I really don't know what happened between you and Adam, and you don't have to tell me. But you two were in love. You were tight…very tight. I remember that. Adam must remember it, and so do you. Nobody would ever forget something like that."

I smiled as my throat closed. As hard as it was to hear this from Lisa, it was also comforting—like those distant memories and all their impact weren't my imagination. Eventually I was able to softly say, "Thanks."

She grinned and laughed. "Not sure what you're thanking me for."

"You're my reality check."

"I thought I was being a bitch."

"Usually." I snickered. "But not this time."

"Ha!" She leaned back and fiddled with her wine glass. "So did you talk to him?"

"I told you I'm telling Juan Carlos tonight."

"No, I mean Adam. Did you talk to Adam?"

Remembering the awkward encounter that morning, I took another drink. "Sort of. There really wasn't time." *Not a lie*, I told myself.

"I'm sure he wants to talk to you."

"Why do you say that?"

"Do you have Alzheimer's or something? He told me that when I saw him in London that one time."

I rolled my eyes. "That was ten years ago."

"So? Like he wouldn't still want to talk?" She gave me a retaliatory eye roll. "That could very well be all he wants. You two are going to be working together, after all."

"Of course I'm going to talk to him…when I have a chance." I tried to sound firm.

"Well, you should. You know, go out to coffee. Clear the air between you two."

"Right," I said. Like it was that easy.

Since the election, Juan Carlos had been on the road. As the political mastermind behind President Logan's election, he was now in high demand. Democratic candidates around the country wanted him to consult on their campaigns. It was a huge moment in his career and a welcome opportunity for him to make a lot of money. I didn't begrudge it at all. The son of Cuban immigrants, Juan Carlos had grown up very modestly, and there was nothing wrong with him profiting from his success.

Because we had been spending so much time together during the campaign, we got close really quickly. Now being thousands of miles apart, we missed each other all the time, but our lives were so busy we could only talk once a day at night. The conversations always had the same arc—first, we talked about what was going on in our lives that day, then we switched over to discussing the news, and finally, without fail, we ended with some heavy phone sex. Juan Carlos was good at phone sex. Very good. Who knew some of the best orgasms of my life would happen when I was by myself? He kept trying to get me to Skype so he'd have a visual, but my American inhibitions held me back.

After Lisa and I polished off the bottle of wine, I took a long bath, and not long after I crawled into bed with a book, Juan Carlos called. He was happy because he'd just landed another big client who was looking to run for governor in New Mexico. When the conversation turned to me, I gave him twenty details about my day at work and nothing about Adam. I didn't have the guts.

It was only when he gave me the perfect opening that I knew I had to stop being a chicken. Juan Carlos asked, "So how was it dealing with the White House Press Corps?"

"Fine. They were nice today. We'll see how it is tomorrow." With a deep breath, I then plunged into the uncharted waters of our relationship. "By the way, that reminds me of something I keep forgetting to tell you." Was that simply a white lie or bald-faced deception? I could feel the shame build inside me, so it had to be the latter.

"What are you forgetting to tell me, *mi reina?*"

Ugh. How could I be his queen when I was such a liar? I felt doubly bad, but I continued, "So did I ever mention I dated a British guy for a while in high school?"

"I can't remember." He chuckled. "All those gringos sound the same to me anyway."

"Very funny." I laughed, which put me more at ease. "Well, this guy happens to be Adam Kincaid…with the BBC."

"The name sounds familiar. I think I've seen him before." His voice rose in disbelief. "You went out with him in high school?"

"Yeah…" With another deep breath of determination, I divulged the pertinent information rapid fire. "He was at my school for a year while his dad was working in Houston. We never kept in touch after he went back to England. I saw him today at the White House for the first time in over fifteen years."

"Must not have been a very serious relationship if you haven't talked to him since high school."

That threw me off. A serious relationship? In a way, Adam and I hadn't been serious at all; it wasn't like we'd been planning on getting married or anything. Yet the relationship itself was significant. As Lisa had said, Adam and I had been tight. Completely perplexed, I tried responding with simple facts. "We were young, and we didn't date for that long. His sister and I still send Christmas cards, though."

"So did you talk to him today?"

"Not really. I was busy."

"Did you see that article in the *Wall Street Journal* about the demise of the British Labor Party?"

"No," I answered, wondering what the hell he was talking about. As I collected my thoughts, Juan Carlos continued on about the article and how he thought he should find some consulting gigs in London. It took me a moment to realize he'd completely moved off the topic of Adam. How had that happened? Somehow I'd managed to make him think that Adam was some insignificant guy I had dated a few times as a teenager. I hadn't done it intentionally, though I supposed a lot of people wouldn't take a typical high school relationship seriously anyway. But what Adam and I'd had was anything but typical.

As Juan Carlos went on about UK politics, I considered bringing Adam up again, but it felt so clumsy to interrupt. Plus, I'd only cause unnecessary suspicion. I told myself I'd correct the record the next time I saw him in person. What a liar I was.

While I was lost in my thoughts, Juan Carlos said, "*Preciosa*, why so quiet?"

"Oh, no good reason." I loved it when he called me "precious one" in Spanish.

"Am I boring you?"

"No, not at all."

"Maybe we should talk about something else? Something more interesting."

"Yeah? Like what?" I smiled, realizing the conversation was heading to its usual, nightly destination.

"We could talk about you taking off your panties."

When Juan Carlos began speaking like a smoldering Latin lover, I forgot about everything, including pesky high school boyfriends. All I could think of was what naughty thing he might say next. I urged him on.

"That's a new topic. Are my panties interesting?" I chuckled.

"Of course. Take them off, though. I like what's underneath better."

Shimmying off my underwear, I said, "Done."

"I bet you look beautiful."

"I wish you were here."

"I wish I was there, too, but I can imagine you lying on your bed, naked and waiting for me. Waiting for me to do things to you."

"Yeah?" I asked in anticipation.

"*Desnudate mi reina. Quiero verte desnuda.*"

Of course I obliged and wiggled off my panties. What woman wouldn't? Phone sex with Juan Carlos was great, and it was downright awesome when he spoke Spanish.

Chapter Three

The following morning, I was determined to remain focused on the two most important things in my life: my boyfriend and my career. Those were solid. I should nurture and enjoy them. Because my job was so all-encompassing, keeping busy with work was easy. And to make sure Juan Carlos didn't leave my mind, I'd occasionally look at his photo or send him a short text. All in all during that morning, I did pretty well at concentrating on what really mattered—until I caught a glimpse of Adam as he walked into the briefing room.

The same simple question from the day before came to mind: *Why?* Why was he in my life again? Was he just passing through? Or was there a reason?

I sneered, a little annoyed with myself for even wondering that. Since I was young, I'd hated the saying that everything happened for a reason—like there was some invisible metaphysical hand maneuvering us through life. If fate existed, it sucked. When I was sixteen, my mom, my sister, and I had been in a horrible car accident. My mom and I had lived. Lauren hadn't. There was no good karmic reason for that.

While I believed in an afterlife that had to be better than a mortal one, I didn't believe God called anyone home early or designed our daily life. Humans had free will, which left our lives up to chance. In my mind, the world was random. Otherwise bad things would never happen to good people, and innocent little girls would never be killed by drunk drivers.

I snuck another look at Adam, whose head was down as he flipped through his reporter's notebook. He was doing his job, just like I was doing mine. *See. No reason*, I told myself. There'd been no cosmic realignment that brought Adam back into my life. I simply needed to have that coffee with him like I'd told Lisa I would. Then I could live in the present when I saw him every day, rather than plunging back into a past that was long gone. I vowed to myself I would talk to him that day.

As usual during the briefing, I ended up fielding some questions from Univision's Antonio De La Fuente. Matt always handed the podium over to me whenever we dealt with the Spanish-speaking press. You could say we were pandering to Latinos whenever I answered questions in Spanish, but I liked to think it was better for everyone if we were accurate and effective in all our communications.

Personally, I liked talking with Antonio because he was friends with Juan Carlos. So when he came up to me after the briefing, I was happy to answer his follow-up questions. He was still a Latin flirt, of course, and he couldn't help but end our conversation with a little wink.

Continuing to smile as he walked away, I looked over to see who was next in line to speak with me. My grin froze when I saw it was Adam, and the surprise caused me to softly exhale. Every sane woman thought he was attractive, but did they also have a physical reaction to him? He stirred something in me. Was it my body remembering what we used to do together, or was it that he'd filled out since he was seventeen and I appreciated the difference? Whatever it was, it felt dangerous.

"I only speak English," he said.

He touched his tie like he'd admitted to a shortcoming, but it only drew my attention to how well-dressed he was. Seeing him so urbane, I didn't believe that English was his only language.

"Really?" I asked.

"Maybe a bit of French."

Shards of forgotten memories reconfigured in my mind, and I could clearly envision his French workbook sitting on my childhood desk. My smile grew. "I think I remember that."

He laughed and gradually locked eyes with mine. He was silent for a few seconds before saying, "Hello, Nicki. It's so good to see you again."

It was a formal yet sincere-sounding introduction, and I responded in kind. "You, too, Adam."

"Your Spanish sounds lovely. Where did you learn to speak it so well?"

"Over the years, and then I…and also my…" Getting into a lengthy discussion about my time in the Peace Corps didn't seem appropriate at the moment, and words completely escaped me when I thought of mentioning Juan Carlos. This was certainly the wrong time and place for that. It was the right moment, though, to pose the question, "We should probably go for coffee one day, don't you think?"

"Yes, that would be nice." He crossed his arms, looking far more comfortable with the situation than me. "But how about lunch instead?"

Lunch. Lunch was longer than coffee. It was more intimate than coffee, too, though it was still completely innocent and professional. I slowly nodded.

"I dare say you're busier than me," he said. "So you tell me when."

"Oh, I think it's always going to be crazy for me around here. We can go whenever."

"How about tomorrow, then?"

"Sure. So far I've only eaten lunch at the White House Mess. I've seen a salad bar around the corner not far from Blair House." I figured a salad bar was lunch, but only a step above coffee as far as intimacy.

"The White House Mess? You need a proper lunch, then. Maybe the Old Ebbitt Grill?"

I knew the name of the restaurant. A Washington institution and hardly a date place. It was the kind of establishment an aristocratic BBC reporter would take an administration official. I played it cool. "It's not too far away, right? I don't know my way around DC yet."

"Just a few streets over."

"Is one o'clock all right?"

"Certainly." He then ripped a page from his notebook and began writing. Handing it over to me, he said, "Here's my mobile number in case you need to get hold of me."

I took the paper and stared at it for a moment. His handwriting was the same, though a little messier. Back at the apartment, I had earlier samples. If I'd wanted to, I could've gone home and compared them. Not that I wanted to. They were tucked safely away with all the other emotionally charged mementos of my life. Best to keep them out of sight.

"Thanks," I said, slowly coming back to the present. "There shouldn't be a problem, but it's good to have. They've handed out my number, right?"

"They have."

"Good." He'd always been tall, but now I felt even smaller around him. Like I was powerless. I looked around what was now an emptying room. "I've gotta go. I'll see you tomorrow, okay?"

"Tomorrow, then," he said, tipping his head to me.

"Bye, Adam." I smiled, but my teeth clenched as I turned around. In order for me to have a professional relationship, there was no other choice but to break the ice. Catching up over lunch was the right thing to do. I couldn't believe it was happening, though. *What have I gotten myself into?*

When I rushed into the restaurant the next afternoon, the cute twenty-something hostess smiled. "Running late?"

"A little."

"What's the name of your party?" she asked, looking down at her register.

"Kincaid. I'm meeting Adam Kincaid."

Her head rose from the book, and I felt her eyes give me a once-over. Obviously she wanted to check out who was meeting the hot guy for lunch. By the quiet nod she gave me, I guessed she wasn't that impressed. A little annoyed, I eyed her back and decided she was too pretty to be smart. I may not have been a supermodel, but I wasn't dumb.

Not wanting to think about it anymore, I asked, "Is he here yet?"

"Yes. I'll take you back."

As she led the way, I followed her stilettos, feeling childishly grumpy. When we arrived at the table, Adam stood up and greeted me with a very professional handshake, though his smile was warm.

I glanced at the hostess, who appeared to observe it all. She turned on her heel, probably thinking it was only a professional lunch, just as she'd thought. *Fuck her.* Though I had to wonder why I cared.

The first few minutes of my lunch with Adam went along easily as we looked over the menu and ordered. When that was done, I peeked at my phone, mostly out of habit, though it also provided me with something to say.

"I'm sorry. I know it's rude to check my phone all the time, but I have to keep up with what's going on." I shrugged. "It's my job."

"No worries. I have to do the same."

"It's funny that we ended up sort of in the same field." I took a sip of water to steady myself.

"Well, I was always going to go into journalism. That's rather boring." He eased back in his seat. "How you got to the White House is a far more interesting story."

"I really don't think it's interesting at all. It's sort of by inertia that I'm here."

"Inertia? What do you mean?"

"A body in motion stays in motion along a straight line, right?"

"So you started doing one thing—working for James Logan—and didn't stop?"

"Pretty much. I was in school at UT for a couple of years—"

"UT?" He cocked his head. "Ah. The University of Texas."

"Exactly. You remember now." I chuckled.

He laughed as well, but his eyes locked on mine again. I noticed the brown in them shown against his green tie. His tone softened a bit. "Oh, I remember."

He remembered. He remembered what? UT? Or did he mean something else? Not wanting to dwell on what was most likely a very insignificant sentence, I started to babble. "When I was a sophomore at UT, Mom remarried. His name is Bill Delano, and he's a successful school superintendent. He really turned around the Houston schools, so he got the opportunity to move to take over the Los Angeles school system. He and Mom moved to California while I was in college. I decided to transfer to the University of Chicago, near my dad. That's where I started interning with President Logan when he was a state senator. He was friends with my dad."

"When did you practice your Spanish?"

"The Peace Corps."

"Really?"

"It was actually at President Logan's urging. After college, I'd been working for him in the governor's press office for a few years. He suggested I go in the Corps, so I joined and was in Mexico for two years. I came back to work for him afterward."

"So you were in the Peace Corps." He leaned forward as if I'd surprised him. "I thought you wanted to go to law school."

"I always expected to — my dad pretty much demanded it, but once I was working in politics, I didn't want to. President Logan had been in the Corps when he was young and recommended it. For me, it was an amazing experience."

"What made you want to live out of the country?"

"The time was right for a break. Mom was in California, and Dad had married his long-term girlfriend, Michelle. Anyway, it felt like it was time for me to do something on my own." I chuckled. "And it was only Mexico. It's right next door. I got to go back home during the year, and both my parents came to visit."

"Hmm. I don't remember Sylvia ever saying you lived in Mexico."

My heart skipped a beat. I always wondered how much Adam's sister told him about me. It wasn't like she knew that much, but even though I hadn't seen her in years, we were pen pals. Did she show Adam my Christmas cards? Had he wanted to keep track of me?

I searched his eyes, looking for an answer, and said, "I kept my apartment in Chicago as my permanent mailing address since I was coming back there anyway."

"So your time in Mexico is where you got your impeccable Spanish?"

"I wouldn't call it impeccable. It's really only passable, but it's enough to get me around."

"Antonio seemed impressed."

"That's because I have an Oaxacan accent. He's from there." I smiled. "Anyway, enough about me. Tell me about your family. I know that Sylvia is in New York."

"Yes, working as an editor at a publishing house specializing in art books."

"You know, I've never asked her, but does she still paint?"

"A little. Not a lot. About halfway through art school, she said she learned enough about art to know that hers sucked compared to everyone else's." He raised a brow. "So now she's a bloody critic and thinks she knows everything."

"Hasn't she always been that way?" I laughed.

"Why yes, she has." He grinned. "And David…you remember my cousin David, don't you?"

Working with the press for so long, I was a pro at keeping an impassive face regardless of the topic, but this wasn't a professional setting. I let out a little gasp that I tried to cover up with a laugh. I couldn't believe he'd brought up David that way. He was teasing me.

How could I ever forget the hot Cockney Brit I'd messed around with one night on a lawn chair? Adam and I probably would've never gotten together had Adam not been so jealous. And David was the same guy my friend Rachel had had a raunchy one night stand with a few years later. Though he was Adam's cousin, David was definitely not an off-limits topic for Lisa, Rachel, and me. He was a legend. "Of course, I remember him."

Adam smirked, and his eyes said exactly what he must have been thinking: *Yeah, I bet you do.* Aloud he said, "David works for Barclays in international finance. He travels often and spends a lot of time in the States, including DC. He says hello, by the way."

"Please tell him hello for me, too." I could feel my cheeks get warm. Oh, how I wished I knew what they'd said in *that* conversation.

"I will."

"And how are your parents? Is your dad still teaching at Cambridge?"

"No, not anymore." He winced and drank from his water glass before he continued, "He's actually rather ill…with pancreatic cancer. My mum spends her days taking care of him."

"Oh, Adam…I'm so sorry." He was silent and grave. I thought he might choke up, so I tried being more matter-of-fact. "When was he diagnosed?"

"A few months ago. The outlook isn't good."

As he fidgeted with his fork, I no longer saw the thirty-three-year-old Adam, a man I wasn't quite sure of. Before me now was Adam, the teenage guy I'd known so well. My heart caved seeing him so sad.

Instinct took over, and I placed my hand over his restless one to calm him. He nodded as I gave him a slight squeeze. He then looked down at our hands and smiled, and I realized what I was doing. *Shit, I'm holding his hand.* I glanced up. *In a restaurant, for crying out loud!* I immediately withdrew my hand and thanked God our food arrived just at that moment.

The conversation became casual, veering from foreign policy to political gossip to silly stories. He even got me laughing so hard at an anecdote about that asshole ABC News reporter Dan Roark, that I started to cry. As I dabbed my eyes, I saw my phone flashing and checked it.

"Is everything okay?" he asked.

"Yeah, I just need to deal with it when I get back. It's going to be another long day and not much sleep tonight."

"So where are you living? Have you found a flat yet?"

I stared at my phone for a minute without saying a word. The time had come to tell him about Juan Carlos. It shouldn't have mattered at all; we'd moved on with our lives, but I became hesitant. It was my turn to fidget, and the information came out slowly. "I'm crashing with Lisa right now. She's doing some post-doc work at NIH and has a place up on Van Ness."

"Lisa? That's nice that you're in the same city again. Do you plan to get a place of your own?"

"No, I…" *Why is this so hard for me?* I forced myself to be forthright. "I'm moving in with my boyfriend."

It was an infinitesimal movement, but I swore Adam's nose twitched. Yet after a second, he smiled. Was he happy for me? At that moment, *I* wasn't. I felt like shit, but why?

"So tell me more about this boyfriend," he said cheerily. "What's his name?"

"Juan Carlos Jimenez. We've been together about a year."

"Really? Juan Carlos Jimenez? I can't say I've met him, though I know of him, of course. Did you two meet on the campaign?"

"Yeah, and we decided to live together last month."

"So why aren't you already moved in?"

"Just busy. He's traveling a ton, and I have no time. We'll make it happen, though."

My voice had wavered a bit while Adam kept a silent smile, and I was awash with shame. I'd now disclosed everything only to realize

I was crazy. If anything, I should've felt guilty for holding hands with any guy other than Juan Carlos. Instead, I felt I was somehow betraying Adam by having another boyfriend. That was insane, especially because it was Adam who had betrayed our relationship when we'd been young.

If we were going to move on from the past, we needed to talk about our new partners. And I knew he had one as well. I didn't want details, though. God, no. I just wanted confirmation he was taken.

Without another thought, I shot the ball out of my court. "So what about you? Who are you dating? You have to be dating someone."

"There's someone. Back in London."

"Someone?" Of course, I could guess who it was. I wasn't above Googling him, and his social life was fodder for the British tabloids.

"Felicity Chambers. She's also with the BBC."

Felicity Chambers may have been with the BBC, but she looked like a Victoria's Secret model. The photos I'd seen of them together came back to me, and trailing not far behind the images in my mind was a sharp pang of jealousy in my gut. I knew the emotion all too well, having spent a good portion of my junior year of high school jealous of his cheerleader girlfriend. It felt like it was happening all over again. I may have been pretty enough with an extra shot of smarts, but I wasn't a Felicity Chambers.

I grasped for something nice. "I think I've seen her on TV. She seems like a good reporter." I actually didn't have any opinion on her reporting skills. What if she sucked, and everyone joked about her? But to stay positive—with an impulsive hope of making everything feel normal between us—I added, "And she's beautiful."

It didn't work. The words had left my mouth, and I only felt worse.

Adam smiled, though. "She's nice."

"Are you two serious?" The question hung in the air, exposing all my insecurities. I was a communications professional, yet I was committing verbal suicide. With every sentence, I sounded more like a creepy ex-girlfriend, and it shouldn't have been that way. I had a boyfriend who was a total catch.

"Serious? Not at the moment. We've been seeing each other for a while, but now that she's back in the UK for good, we've put things on hold, so to speak." He cleared his throat. "You know. Long-distance relationships are difficult."

My eyes widened. Well, what in the hell was I supposed to say to that? Had he meant to say it like I knew something about the subject, or was it just a figure of speech? Of course I knew long-distance relationships were difficult. That was one of the reasons I had never let Adam and me have one.

He looked around the room. Maybe he wasn't enthused by the conversation either. My phone vibrated, saving us both. It was Matt, so I knew it must be important. I apologized and took the call at the table, trying to keep talk of President Logan to a minimum. An inadvertent slip of information to the press—even just to Adam—was the last thing I needed.

When I finished, I had my marching orders from Matt. While I didn't mind the work, I didn't like leaving so abruptly. I sighed. "I'm very sorry. I need to get back to the office. Something's happened."

"Anything I might find interesting?" He smiled reassuringly. "That was a joke. I don't want it to be like that between us. You don't have to tell me anything if it will make you uncomfortable."

I snorted at that.

"What? What did I say?" he asked.

I shook my head. "Like some of the conversation today hasn't already been uncomfortable."

"I'm sorry." He laughed, seeming to genuinely appreciate my candor. "That wasn't my intention."

"I know, and I don't want it that way either." I wasn't sure what way I wanted it, but any more of this awkwardness would kill me. I grabbed my purse from the back of my chair. "Sorry. This isn't the best time for me to leave, but I've got to get back."

"Nicki, before you do, I need to know something. Please. It's important."

"What's that?"

"Well, when I took this assignment, I told my boss in London we were once school chums. I left it at that, though. If I told them anything else, I might not have been allowed to take the position. So I need to know…what have you said?"

So he'd called us "school chums." *How quaint. How British. How amazingly inaccurate!* I'd lost my virginity to him. We'd fucked around like only horny, angst-ridden, lovesick teenagers could do. We'd once pledged our undying love to each other. *School chums?* Even my half-ass disclosures were better than that. And wasn't "chum" the name of some kind of nasty fish? So I was a chum to him?

Bastard, I nearly muttered out loud, but I shrugged it off. "I told Matt I knew you in high school and that we went out. Juan Carlos knows as well. I agree it's not something we need gossip about."

"Precisely."

I stared him down as the same question reverberated inside me, wanting to get out: *Why?* Why had he taken the job—practically lying in order to do it? I understood why the BBC likewise wouldn't want a White House correspondent who'd ever been romantically involved with a presidential press secretary. He could go soft on the administration or let something slip. So why had he risked his job? Was it just to take a choice assignment at the White House?

Whatever the answer, I wasn't going to find out that afternoon. His eyes gave nothing away, and my phone buzzed again.

"Thanks for lunch," I said, seizing my escape. "I'll see you tomorrow."

"Yes. Tomorrow," he said with a smile.

That night when I got home, Lisa didn't even wait for me to put down my bag before she pounced. Leaning against the foyer wall, she asked, "So how was lunch with Adam?"

I dropped my bag on the floor, where it landed with a thud. "Fine, but you know I did other things today, too—like work, for example."

"Whatever. Tell me what happened."

"We ate lunch, and we caught up on our lives."

"And?"

"It was a little awkward—"

"A little?"

"Okay." I laughed. "At times, it was incredibly awkward."

"That's more realistic."

"But we had a nice time, and there was no big revelation." Hanging my winter coat in the closet, I sighed. "From what I can tell, he has a girlfriend, and I have a boyfriend, and we simply happen to work in the same field." I shut the door. "Thus ends the story."

"So it's just a coincidence that you're in daily contact again?"

"I think so." I checked my phone to see a waiting voicemail from Juan Carlos. "If you don't mind, I don't want to talk about it anymore."

"Hmpf." She crossed her arms in dissatisfaction.

"What?"

"Nothing."

"What are you getting at? Like this is fate?"

"Did I say that?"

"You're a scientist, and I *know* you don't believe in fate."

"I don't."

"But now you don't believe in coincidence either?" I threw my hand on my hip.

"Yes, I'm a scientist. Of course I don't believe in fate, but true coincidences are highly rare." She turned around and walked to the living room, grumbling from behind, "I believe in cause and effect."

Alone in the foyer, I caught sight of myself in the mirror above the table where we stashed our purses and bags. The dark circles under my eyes caused me to take a step closer to get a better look. With each passing year, the person in the mirror had been slowly changing from Nicki, the girl I'd been all my life, to Nicole, the woman I now was. Lines had begun to permanently mark my face. I grimaced. Years of working stressful political jobs at a breakneck pace had taken their toll. I looked old.

Did Adam think I'd aged? That Felicity seemed younger than me. Adam was my age, and men liked younger women.

Staring at myself in the mirror, a memory floated back to me—one that I'd done my best to keep forgotten. It was from the night before Adam had moved back to England, when he'd asked, *"Nicki, will we ever speak to each other again?"*

"I…don't know," I said. "I guess never say never, but it's kind of unlikely. Our lives are going to be very different. I mean, we really do live a world apart. An ocean apart, anyway."

His silence was deafening. So much so that I felt like I had to make an offer, but it was so improbable, I was comfortable saying it. "Maybe. Maybe, if we were living in the same city."

"As you said, that's probably not going to happen."

"Probably not."

Yet now the improbable had happened. The adult woman in the mirror stared me down with no answers to my questions. It was frustrating. When it came to Adam, I might as well have been a teenager again.

Chapter Four

For the next few weeks, I stuck to my old life — a life without Adam in it. I focused on Juan Carlos, and at work I concentrated on the tasks at hand. For the hour or so I was in the same room with Adam every day, I ignored him. Yes, he would creep into my mind, but I'd quickly force out any thought of him. It was simply a coincidence we were both in DC to do our jobs. There was nothing more to it.

One Friday, I got stuck talking with Dan Roark after the briefing. He was handsome in that star-quarterback kind of way, and he used his looks to get in good with female sources. I always thought there was something slimy about him, but I had to be fair to everyone. That meant I had to listen to him drone on about rumors he'd heard about investigative hearings on the Hill, even though I knew he was only creating gossip to see what my reaction would be.

I was just about to extricate myself from the conversation when, out of the corner of my eye, I saw Adam approach Matt and say, "Matthew, do you have a minute? It'll be short."

How I wanted to hear what Adam was going to say and how Matt would react. I didn't think Matt would bring up high school, but what if he did? If I was going to listen to their conversation, I would have to keep talking with Dan. *Yuck.*

With a smile, I persevered and told him a lie that would keep him talking for hours. "I really don't know the Hill that well. How long have you been covering Congress? It's really fascinating."

Dan gave me a smug smile. *Great.* He thought I was flirting with him, but as he went on about his fabulous career, I tuned him out and listened to Adam and Matt.

Matt gave Adam a backslap and said, "Sure, I'll talk today, but we should probably get coffee or something soon—and definitely before we head overseas."

"Wonderful. I'll speak to your assistant to arrange a time. I need some immediate help, though."

"What's that?"

"I'm working on a story on the new administration and China," Adam said, tapping his reporter's notebook. "I was wondering who the best person is to talk to about China's devalued currency. Is there someone you recommend at Treasury?"

"Now, Adam, don't put words in our mouth." Matt chuckled. "I don't believe the president has made any official comments about the value of China's currency."

"Ah, that's part of my story," he said with a smile. "The president mentioned it during the campaign as a major economic issue for the US."

"I gotta tell you. This is not at the top of Treasury's mind right now. Hell, we're still working to get the Secretary confirmed by the Senate." Matt then looked over his shoulder and said, "Let me see what I can do for you. How about talking to Nicole? She handles all the wonky stuff."

My stomach clenched when I heard Matt say my name. I didn't want to talk to Adam, especially with Matt standing by, but there was no way to get out of it. I cut Dan off mid-sentence and sent him on his way. At least it was an abrupt enough ending to show I hadn't been flirting.

I turned to Matt. "Excuse me? What do you need me for?"

"Adam here needs some background on the president's thinking about the Chinese currency." His voice was flat, but his eyes were mirthful as he added, "I believe you two know each other."

"Yeah…" I said. So Matt was going to torment me about Adam. *Wonderful.*

Adam seemed unruffled by the comment. "Yes, we've known each other for a while."

"Great. No introductions are necessary," Matt said, slapping Adam's back again. Then he motioned toward the door. "Nicole, I need to leave. Can you make sure to cover that meeting for me at noon?"

"Sure," I said as he walked away. I loved my boss, but at that moment…not so much. I looked up at Adam. "Hi."

"Hello." He smiled. "How are you? Shame we haven't been able to talk this week."

"Yes…it's been busy. Is there something you needed besides this China question?"

Adam was quiet and simply rolled his pen between his fingers as if he hadn't heard me, so I launched into work. That was the appropriate thing to do and the proper topic. "As a candidate, President Logan often spoke of his belief—a widely held belief, I might add—that China artificially manipulates the yuan in order to unfairly bolster its exports."

"It's not so widely held. The Chinese government disagrees."

I hadn't really expected a retort from him. Well, if he wanted to debate, we could do that. "And your own government agrees. Great Britain has long concurred with the assessment that the yuan is undervalued."

"Yes, the British government agrees, but that doesn't make it so. If it's such a pressing issue, why isn't President Logan working on it right now? What does he plan to do?"

"At the appropriate time, no doubt, the president will address the issue again. When that will be or what it might look like, I don't know."

Adam scribbled notes as I spoke and kept his head down as he asked, "Does he believe that China's currency manipulation is contributing to the global recession?"

"There are many factors that have created the recession. The president is simply concerned about any effect China's monetary actions are having on American jobs. The trade deficit impacts the lives of working men and women by sending production overseas."

"With regard to China, what is he planning to do?"

"President Logan will always act to save American jobs." I cracked a smile as I said the words. It was a platitude I'd repeated a hundred times, but somehow saying it to Adam made me realize it sounded kind of corny.

He looked up from his notebook, and his eyes lit up on noticing I was laughing at myself. "Does that include trade protections that the WTO might take issue with?"

"I think I told you I don't know what the president will do." I laughed. It always had been fun debating him.

"It looks like we've both done our jobs."

"What do you mean?"

"I asked the tough questions, and you responded that you don't know when clearly you do."

"What do you think I know?"

"You tell me." He gave me a playful look, inviting me to volley back at him. "I'm not sure."

No one could say we were flirting. After all, we were talking about the Chinese currency. Could there be anything less romantic or sexy? Yet it didn't feel like a dry work conversation to me. It was playful and fun, and I needed to cut it off.

"I have to go," I said. "I'm sorry that I wasn't more help. I'll have someone follow up with you. Bye." Turning on my heel, I fled the room.

On Saturday night, Adam was the furthest thing from my mind. Juan Carlos was in town, and a big group of us had ventured out to a great tapas place in Adams Morgan. It had good food, strong mojitos, and a big dance floor for salsa dancing. The whole vibe of the place was a precursor to sex.

And when Juan Carlos danced with me, sex was all I could think about. He was an amazing dancer. The worst dance partners were always those who couldn't lead. I was a feminist, but damn it, I couldn't stand a man who couldn't lead on the dance floor. It was so frustrating, and I'd end up taking over because they were so lame. There was none of that with Juan Carlos. He whipped you around with an authority that just made you want to follow him anywhere, and he could make even the worst dance partner look good.

That night we danced and had a great time. Occasionally, I'd look down and watch his hips swivel, which of course made me think of the reunion sex we'd be having later. It had been a while since we were in the same city.

When the DJ switched the music to a slow song, he smiled at me. "Do you want a break, or should we continue?"

"I could use a break," I said, lifting my hair up to fan myself.

With his hand around my waist, Juan Carlos began to lead me over to our table, where Lisa and the rest of our party were waiting. He stopped in his tracks when a man walked directly in front of us, blocking our way. I looked up to see who the asshole was, and my mouth gaped open.

"Hello," said Adam, standing before us with a smile. He offered his hand to Juan Carlos. "Adam Kincaid. You're Juan Carlos Jimenez, correct?"

"Yes," Juan Carlos replied, shaking his hand. "It's nice to meet you. The BBC, right? I've seen you before."

"Yes, I'm with the BBC," Adam said as he withdrew his hand.

I'd told Juan Carlos about my lunch with him, stressing that Adam had a girlfriend, a very public one in fact, but Juan Carlos still pulled me in tighter. "I believe you and Nicki know each other."

"Yes, we've known each other for a while," said Adam matter-of-factly.

"Hi, Adam," I said, not quite mustering up a reciprocal smile.

He turned to Juan Carlos. "Do you mind if I have a quick dance?"

Holy shit. Adam wanted to dance with me. Normally I hated the ritual of a man breaking in to dance. The guy always asked the other guy, rather than you, and all of sudden you weren't in the twenty-first century anymore. You were back in the nineteenth, and you were chattel. That night, though, I was happy to have someone running interference for me.

Juan Carlos studied Adam for the briefest moment. I couldn't tell if he thought Adam was harmless or just thought refusing him was a stupid move, even if he really wanted to. Regardless, he didn't help me out. He simply shrugged and asked me to make the decision. "Nicki?"

"Sure," I said as nonchalantly as possible. "I'll meet you back at the table in a minute."

Juan Carlos squeezed my hand and then grinned at Adam. "Come over to our table when you're done."

"Thanks. I'll do that," Adam said.

As I watched Juan Carlos walk away, I felt Adam take my hand, and before I knew it, I was in his arms. With an incredibly romantic song playing in the background, I placed my hand on his shoulder. The bizarre scene left me speechless, so I lifted my eyes to see what Adam thought of all this.

"How are you?" he asked with a cheeky grin.

"Good." I swallowed, searching for small talk. "Who are you here with?"

"David. I'm sure he'd like to talk to you."

"Of course. David." As if events weren't crazy enough, throw in the cousin, too.

"He's in town for a meeting at the SEC on Monday."

"Where are you two sitting?"

Adam surveyed the room, stopped, and then shook his head with a laugh. "It looks like we're sitting with you now."

"What do you mean?"

"David appears to have joined your table."

"What?" It came out a little too loud, though I didn't care. I was in a panic. I furiously craned my neck over the crowd to find the table, but I was too short.

"He's sitting next to Lisa. I apologize in advance if he makes a pass at her."

"Are you crazy? That's the last thing I'm worried about. What is he going to say?" Then a worse thought hit me. "What is *she* going to say? Oh my God."

"Don't worry. David won't cause a scene. He's got things under control." Adam peered over at the table again. "He'll take care of Lisa. I'm sure he's laying on the Cockney charm and everyone's getting on just fine. I see Juan Carlos is laughing."

That was reassuring. Sort of. I gave him a quick smile but remained quiet. Maybe if I said nothing, the music would finish more quickly. Unfortunately, the silence made me concentrate on the lyrics. As I rested my hand on Adam's shoulder, which seemed much broader than I'd remembered it, I realized the words were far too sexy for a dance with Adam. Thank God he didn't know Spanish.

I had to say something to start a conversation, so I stated the obvious. "We're dancing."

"Yes, we are." He took a breath and said, "I don't believe we ever did that."

"I don't think so either." I laughed.

He arched a brow, which seemed to suggest all the things we *did* do together. I had to look away as my mind raced through some very naughty memories.

"Nicki, you're blushing. I think I know why."

I tried playing dumb. "Why?"

"Because you're thinking what I'm thinking."

I'd always been a sucker for that special twinkle in his eye when he would tease me, like he was onto me and couldn't wait to see what I'd do next. That night, the twinkle was in full force, and I gave in with a sigh. "In an effort to keep things from being awkward between us, I'll say those were fun times."

"I thought so," he said in a more serious tone.

The twinkle vanished as he splayed his hand across my back and pulled me toward him. I was only an inch closer, but it was enough for my body to realize who it was next to. Staring at his chest, I saw Adam was right there and ready for the taking. My smile faded as crazy pheromones took over. All I wanted was to mash my body against his and feel him once more.

I looked up, curious what he was thinking. When I saw at least a kiss was on his mind, my lips parted in a mix of fear and want. As if the universe swooped in to save me from myself, the song finally ended.

"I should get back," I mumbled. "Thanks for the dance."

"I think I get another dance since I only got half of the last one."

Stunned by his demand and my complete inability to say no to the guy, I gave him a silent nod. I hadn't totally lost my senses to dormant teenage hormones, though. I made sure there was a safe distance between us, and somehow the separation allowed me to be direct.

"Adam, what are you doing?"

"To be quite honest, I'm not sure."

He seemed candid, but I couldn't handle any more ambiguity. I needed an answer to the question that had been bugging me for weeks. "Why did you take the White House job?"

"Why do you think?"

"I don't know. I can't tell."

"For the record, it definitely wasn't because I thought I might get some kind of special access to the Logan administration because of you."

"That thought really never entered my mind. You wouldn't do something like that." It was true. I never thought he was trying to use our ties professionally. That just wasn't Adam.

"You know me well."

He smiled and pulled me closer to him—closer than even a few minutes before. The woolly scent of his sport coat drifted toward me. I could've easily slipped into the moment and rested my head on his chest, but that was wrong for so many reasons. At once, I stepped back and announced in as firm a voice as I could find, "I have a boyfriend. Here. In this room."

"I know." It came out bitterly, but his next words were softer. "Yet surely we could be friends again."

I looked at him askance. "We were never *just* friends."

"No…we weren't, but we could give it a try."

There were many reasons why Adam and I had broken up before he'd returned to England, just as there were many reasons why we hadn't kept in touch. A paramount one was that I hadn't wanted to only be his friend. I couldn't bear the thought of hearing about his new girlfriends and life after I'd been left behind. Yes, it had been selfish and childish, but back then, I'd been a self-centered child. Plus, I'd been through enough pain to last a lifetime. I knew better than to pile more on.

I shook my head. "I should go back."

Without another word or look, I dropped his hand and headed to our group. I managed to walk in a straight line, but it was an effort. I was dizzy with the thought that Adam might very well still be interested in me and felt the need to confirm it to myself. *That is what he sort of said in a non-committal way, right?*

I spotted the table, though it was hardly a sanctuary. David sat right between Juan Carlos and Lisa. Juan Carlos was laughing as David appeared to give an animated retelling of a story with his arm resting around the back of Lisa's chair. When David let it slide against her back, she shot him a look. She then noticed me coming toward her, and her eyes were aflame. I knew exactly what she was thinking, because I was wondering it as well: *What in the hell is going on?*

As I approached the table, Juan Carlos rose to help me with my chair. Smiling, he kissed my cheek. *"Hola, preciosa."*

"Thanks for saving my seat." I gave him a peck back, fully conscious that Adam was only a foot away.

David stood up and extended his hand to me. "Hello. You probably don't remember me. I'm Adam's cousin, David Bates."

"Oh, I remember you." I smiled, thinking Juan Carlos really didn't need to know about my little make-out session with David in Lance's backyard all those years ago. I tried to signal that I barely knew the guy. "It's nice to meet you again."

Juan Carlos laughed. "David is hilarious. He tells the best stories."

I kept smiling but only nodded. I figured the less I said about knowing David, the better.

As I sat down, Adam found a chair on the other side of Lisa, and David said, "Adam, Dr. Lisa Roberts. You remember her, don't you?"

"Hello, Lisa." Adam extended his hand to her. "I believe I last saw you in London."

"Hello." She gave him a perfunctory smile and muttered, "It's been a while." She then glared at me with a silent *What the fuck?*

I answered by gulping my sangria. Thankfully, Juan Carlos was far more interested in the conversation with his friends across the table, who were debating the best soccer team in Mexico. Adam's attention had likewise been grabbed by a young Hill staffer, who'd had enough smarts to realize the BBC White House correspondent was sitting next to him. I tuned out as soon as I heard the guy say, "My boss, Senator Lexford, sits on the Foreign Relations Committee."

While I sat studying my drink, David moved a little closer to Lisa. His Cockney accent became sultry. "You know, Lisa, you're beautiful—like a Nubian princess."

"You have got to be kidding me."

"Not at all."

"Do you even know where Nubia is?"

"Africa, I suppose."

"You say it like it's a small place. Africa is a friggin' continent."

"What does it matter? It's a compliment, princess."

"Princess? I bet that's something you call all your women."

"Only if they're gorgeous like you."

"And the black ones are Nubian princesses?"

"Not all of them. You're special."

"Please." She gave him a look like she'd just sucked on a lemon. "Don't even start that shit with me."

"Shit? I'm not talking shit. You're a pretty little thing. Smooth chocolate skin, striking face, and lovely dark eyes."

She snorted. "You're going to have to work a lot harder than that."

"I like a challenge."

I could barely hear her whisper, "You've got to be kidding me. The last time I saw you, you ended up fucking Rachel, one of my best friends. Not to mention…" She gave a sharp nod toward me.

"All ancient history."

"You're crazy if you think I'm next."

"Oh, you're still a feisty one. I remember that about you. I like feisty." He waggled his eyebrows. "I'm good with feisty. Just give me a chance. You won't regret it."

"Are you for real?" She shook her head.

"Oh yes, and I'm not going away."

While Lisa and David continued their banter, Maria Ines Ortega, Juan Carlos's friend from college, sidled up next to me. "Hey, Nicki."

"Hi." Maria Ines always made me grin. She was perpetually on the make, and as a gorgeous Colombian, she was quite successful in her conquests. She had the best tales to tell. "How are you?"

"I'm great." She nodded over to Adam, who was still stuck talking to the staffer. "Juan Carlos says Adam's a friend of yours. He said he has a girlfriend. Is that right?"

"Yes, he does," I said slowly. I peered over at him. "Her name is Felicity Chambers. She also works for the BBC."

"Probably one of those horsey-looking British chicks," said Maria Ines. Tossing her hair, she stuck out her chest. "He needs a night with me. He's probably never been with a real woman."

Since I'd been with Adam when I was only seventeen, I couldn't object — not that I really wanted the conversation to go any further. I did wonder what Adam would do if Maria Ines worked her magic on him, though. Men flocked to her the way women fell over themselves for David. I considered it a test.

"Go talk to him," I said.

"I will."

I dreaded the next question, but it was the polite one for me to ask. "Do you want me to introduce you?"

"No, thanks." She winked. "I can handle it."

She left me behind and pulled up a chair between Adam and the staffer. Turning her back on the poor guy, she effectively iced him out as she began talking with Adam. It was a matter of seconds before her trademark eye-fucking commenced. I looked away. I didn't want to see Adam's reaction.

For the rest of the night, I drank sangria and checked my watch, hoping that I would get out of there before it all exploded in my face. Of course, home would be no better because I'd be alone with Juan Carlos and my guilt, and when he left the next day, I'd be just as confused by Adam and get a lecture from Lisa. I began to plot a Sunday afternoon trip into the office just to avoid my personal life.

Fortunately, because there was such a large group at the table, I didn't have to say much. Juan Carlos held court just as he always did. He was a charismatic guy, and people were drawn to him. Plus, he was the most successful campaign consultant in America right now and sitting in a popular restaurant in DC. The man was going to have admirers and customers. I welcomed the conversations as a diversion from Adam, though occasionally I'd peek to see if Maria Ines was making any headway. I couldn't tell, but close to two in the morning, I did overhear David ask for Lisa's phone number.

She gave him a deadpan look. "After everything I've said to you tonight, you want to call me?"

"Of course, love. Why not?"

"Whatever." She yawned. "Adam is a reporter. He should be able to track it down."

"Still playing hard to get?" David said with a smile.

"Oh, I'm not playing at all. I am hard to get, especially for you."

He leaned over and gave her the quickest peck on the cheek before he rose from his seat. She touched where his lips had landed, but rather than scolding him, she gave me a stern look. I was going to get a talking to.

Adam and David said their farewells, and curiosity got the best of me. I studied Adam's goodbye to Maria Ines. She leered at him, and he nodded and turned away.

As he spoke to the Hill staffer, Maria Ines came over to me and said, "Either he's in love with his girlfriend or he's gay, because he wouldn't flirt with me." She glared at Adam. "He's really not that attractive, you know."

"Right," I said with a nod. *Crazy woman.*

When Adam and David made their way to Juan Carlos and me to say goodbye, Juan Carlos stood up, and there was much backslapping. *Great. They're all buddies now.*

David beamed down at me. "Good seeing you again, Nicki. You're gorgeous as ever."

I had to grin. He was too charming not to respond. "Thanks, David. It was good to see you, too."

Adam followed up with a pleasant but far more professional, "Good night, Nicki. I suppose I'll see you on Monday."

My giddiness over David's charm faded into a nervous smile for Adam. "Yes. Monday. Good night."

I stared at them as they walked away. Two tall, well-dressed guys standing out among the crowd of sweaty salsa dancers. I watched a second too long, though — before he got to the door, Adam turned around and caught me. His eyes met mine, and I looked away. *Damn it.*

As we went home in a cab, Juan Carlos announced, "It's nice that you're friends with Adam. He seems like a good guy. Maria Ines seemed to like him."

"Yeah," I said, looking out the window at the lights as we sped down Connecticut Ave. *Friends.* There was that word again. I searched for something emotionally innocuous so I wouldn't lie but also not raise any red flags. "It was good to see him."

The night that had started with me dying to get my boyfriend alone so I could pounce on him ended with me dreading my bedroom. With no place in DC yet, Juan Carlos always spent his nights in town with me. Lisa's apartment had three bedrooms and two baths, so we had ample privacy and could be as loud as we wanted. There I was, though, silently going through the motions of sex with my beloved boyfriend and hardly enjoying the moment. Adam had ruined it for me, or I had ruined it for myself. Both were true.

When it was over, Juan Carlos curled up behind me. Despite the intimacy, my mind was elsewhere. I looked out into the darkness and remembered again the night before Adam had moved back to England. The second part of our conversation came back to me—a promise I'd clung to, though it would've been better forgotten. Deep down, I had always admitted I would be mortally crushed if it never came true.

"But what if…what if I was thirty-five and still single? Could I contact you then?" Adam asked.

What he described seemed unimaginable. I couldn't really comprehend what it would be like to be thirty-five. And the idea that he would ever be single was ridiculous. I said yes. "In the highly unlikely event that was the case, I'd say sure."

"Really?"

"You've got to admit, it's probably not going to happen."

He happily kissed my nose. "Maybe, maybe not."

Of course, life hadn't worked out that way. We weren't thirty-five yet, and neither of us was single. Instead, we'd been thrown together sooner than expected—too soon, or maybe too late. Adam might have had a hand in making it happen, but his intentions weren't clear, not even to him. The situation wasn't what we'd imagined, and it could end badly. Most of all for me.

The following morning, Juan Carlos and I took a shower together as I tried to rally myself for him. He didn't seem to notice I was out of sorts. Either he was distracted by the sex or the flight he had to catch to Seattle at noon.

After he caught his cab to Dulles, I went upstairs with my plan to give Lisa the sorry-I-gotta-run-goodbye and then flee to the safety of the office. She wouldn't hear of it.

"Oh no you don't," she said as she blocked the path to my room. "You stay right here. We need to talk."

"Tonight."

"No way. I'm dying to know what you and Adam talked about when you were dancing!"

"I'm kind of dying to know also."

"What do you mean?"

"It was odd."

She pointed to the living room. "Sit. Tell me what happened, for once, between you and Adam. Word for word."

"Okay…"

After we plopped down on the sofas, she said, "Now, don't leave anything out."

"All right." What a fib. I retold her everything we'd said, but not what I'd felt. I left out the moments I had wanted to kiss him and all that. No need to go into details that would only get me in trouble.

After I finished, she twisted her mouth as she appeared to mull it all over. Finally, she said, "So he says he's not sure why he took the job? Like it could be you or it could be the work."

"Yup."

"But he wants to be friends."

"That's what he said." I frowned and muttered, "Not my idea."

"You still don't want to be friends with him?"

"Honestly, I don't know if I'd be good at being friends with him."

"Well, that's a warning sign…"

"Warning of what?"

"That you're still interested in him, silly."

"Well, yeah, in a way," I mumbled. My tone strengthened. "But I have Juan Carlos, and he's great."

"Juan Carlos is a good man who is good to you. Not to mention he's gorgeous. Hell, even his name is sexy. Any woman would want to be with him." She waggled her finger at me. "Don't you forget that."

"Believe me, I won't. I love him."

"Good." She looked out the window for a moment, then shook her head. "But Adam…he's still interested in you, though he has a girlfriend."

"Let's not get too carried away with his level of 'interest.' The guy says he wants to be my friend."

"Hmm." She tapped her fingers against her lips. "Maybe this is all one big test for him."

"What do you mean?"

"Well, he has a girlfriend, but he's still interested in you. He wants to see if there's still anything there between you. The girlfriend is his safety net. She's the control group in the experiment."

"You are such a scientist."

"But I'm probably right."

"Huh? You really think he's calculated it that way?"

"Maybe not fully consciously, but it kind of looks that way."

"Maybe." It did sort of make sense, but I was wary. "You realize our jobs are at stake here. Nothing can really happen between us. It's highly unethical, especially for him, and for me, it's a political scandal."

"Yeah, your boss *is* the president of the United States," she said, pointedly stating the obvious.

"I can't be screwing around with the press, but you think I should be friends with him?"

"Of course. Otherwise you'll never know."

"But Adam has never even flirted with me, never even paid me a compliment."

"Really? Not even something like, 'You look good'?"

"Nope. He's been very professional."

"That's a good thing, right? You don't want him hitting on you and further complicating things."

"True." I smirked. "But maybe it's because I'm not a Nubian princess."

She covered her eyes with uncharacteristic drama. "Don't get me started with David. That guy is crazy."

"Crazy but cute, and Rachel and I can vouch for him." I punctuated it with a wink.

"Don't remind me," she grumbled.

Chapter Five

For the next few weeks, Adam and I were friendly when we saw each other, but no more than when we interacted with anyone else in the briefing room. As curious as I was about him, I was happy not to have my workweek thrown into emotional upheaval. Maybe he felt the same way.

I often pondered on what his life was like outside of work. Did Felicity visit him often? What was she like? When I was on the phone with Juan Carlos, was Adam talking with Felicity? And what did she know of me? Everything or nothing? The ruminations never lasted too long, as the stomach-churning jealousy made me physically sick.

One Saturday morning, I was at work again when Juan Carlos called to tell me his flight had been canceled. There was a late winter storm headed east, and he'd already gotten caught in it in Chicago. As I resigned myself to a weekend of work instead of fun, my phone buzzed again with a New York number I didn't know. Working with the media, that happened all the time, so I figured it was a reporter.

"This is Nicole," I answered.

"Nicki? Hello. This is Sylvia Kincaid."

At first my eyes bugged out in surprise, but then I smiled. I'd always loved Adam's sister. "Sylvia! It's so good to hear from you. How did you get my number?"

"Adam gave it to me. I hope you don't mind."

"No, not at all." The thought of Adam giving my number away, even to his sister, struck me as sort of funny.

"Oh good. So listen. I'm sure your weekend is already packed, but I'm on the train right now heading to DC. I have some work there on Monday and Tuesday, and I wanted to make sure I wasn't delayed by the storm. Could you squeeze me in for brunch tomorrow or even coffee sometime?"

For a moment I wondered if she would bring Adam along, but on second thought, I doubted it. Sylvia had always been very careful to keep our friendship separate from my relationship with her brother.

"I'd love to see you, and yes, brunch would be fine. Where should we meet?"

The following morning, I met Sylvia at a Belgian restaurant near Dupont Circle. When we were in high school, she was a shy little Goth with more fashionable clothes than anyone else in Bellaire, Texas. She still had black hair, though the dye job was better now, and she was still the best-dressed woman in the restaurant. The French waiter was all over her because she flirted with him *en français*.

When he left the table, I said, "He's a hottie."

"He is." Her eyes lingered on him as he walked away. "I have a thing for waiters. Half of them are artists and actors."

"Are you seeing anyone?"

"I'm dating, but no one seriously." She smiled. "Tell me about your bloke. Adam mentioned you're dating someone."

In a way, I would've loved to have heard that conversation, and in a way not. I made the best of it by smiling. "His name is Juan Carlos Jimenez."

"His name is fantastic. Do you have a picture? Adam said he's famous, but I don't really follow politics. Sorry."

"That's okay. I'm not sure I'd call him famous, but he's been very successful lately." I pulled my phone from my bag and showed her my favorite photo of Juan Carlos and me.

"Aw…what a lovely couple," she said, leaning across the table to get a better look. "He's quite handsome. Have you been together for a while?"

"Not that long. We met on the campaign last year."

"It's good to see you happy." She nodded. "I hope you know I mean that."

"I do," I said, touching my heart. "You've always been understanding."

"I just never wanted what happened between you and Adam to end us being friends."

"I appreciate that."

"Of course, Adam has moved on as well." She waived her hand. "Now with that Felicity."

"What about her?" I had to know what she meant.

"Well, I'm not betraying any confidences in saying Mummy and I don't like her. She's gauche."

That made me laugh. "I distinctly remember your father not liking me, probably for the same reason."

"Now, that's not true. He liked you. He just didn't think you were right for Adam, especially when you two were so young. Regardless, he's very impressed with you now."

"What do you mean?"

"Since Daddy's been so ill, he watches a lot of television. He never misses Adam, so he sees you often when you speak at the White House. Daddy thinks you're very accomplished."

Admittedly, I was a little bitter about Adam's father. It's not like he'd broken us up, and both my parents had also let me know Adam and I were too young. Yet I'd always gotten the feeling that I wasn't quite good enough to date the son of a viscount or whatever his title.

Still, I smiled and said, "That's nice to hear." Then I couldn't help myself. "What does he think of Felicity?"

"Daddy? Oh, he's a little indifferent. He's still upset with Adam for breaking up with Muff."

"Ah, Muff. He was with her for a while wasn't he?" Like I didn't know…I'd spent countless hours online stalking Adam's relationship with Lady Mary Selbourne, a.k.a. "Muff." I had always liked to call her Twat whenever I read about them together. They had dated for years but then broke it off.

"Yes, he split with her two years ago now when the drumbeat of marriage got too loud. Frankly, I think he would've done it a lot sooner, but it took a while for him to get the courage."

"Courage? Why's that?"

"I do believe he loved her in a way, but I think he also felt he was supposed to be with a woman like her, not that she was the one he actually wanted."

"Oh." I picked at my food for a moment, trying not to smile. Sylvia was telling me so many things that made me happy when they really shouldn't. When I looked up, I switched to a safer topic. "So tell me about your job."

There was no talk of Adam until the end of the meal, but then she really put me on the spot. "What are your plans for the rest of the day?" she asked.

"Actually, not much. I always have work to do, but I was in the office yesterday. Juan Carlos is still out of town, so I suppose I'll watch some TV while the snow falls. What are you doing?"

"Adam and I are going to the Sackler Gallery. I'm friends with the director, and he's arranged for us to have a special viewing of some works that aren't on display. Do you want to come along?"

"Um…"

"I don't want it to be awkward for you, so please don't feel like you have to."

It felt like another test. Could I spend the afternoon with Adam in a platonic setting? I knew I should be able to say yes, so I took a breath and smiled. "A little awkward maybe, but it would be fun. Thanks for asking me."

An hour later, Sylvia and I climbed out of a cab in front of the Arthur M. Sackler Gallery and Freer Gallery of Art. Well, I was the one who climbed. With it snowing outside on a Sunday morning, I tumbled out in a ski jacket, jeans, and snow boots, whereas Sylvia daintily stepped out in her chic black hat, long coat, and boots that looked treacherous on the ice.

I spotted Adam standing to the left outside the front entrance. He was dressed like me in a parka with jeans, and he smiled as we walked toward him. I had a feeling he hadn't known I was coming along.

When we reached him, Sylvia said, "Hiya. I asked Nicki to join us."

"Brilliant. Hello," he said with an appreciative nod.

"Hi."

His grin widened, and he reached out and tousled the pompom on my stocking cap. The twinkle was back in his eye, and I felt it in my heart. When we were in high school, he used to touch my ponytail the same way. Embarrassed, I took off the hat.

He gestured to the museum door. "Shall we?"

While Sylvia spoke with a woman at the front desk, Adam and I were both quiet. He stared at the art in the entrance area, and I decided it was time for a quick text to Juan Carlos. He knew I'd had brunch with Sylvia that morning, but I needed to tell him about Adam.

Had brunch with Sylvia. Now at the Sackler w/ her.
Adam is here, too. Hope you're having a good day. I love you.

As usual, his response was quick.

Sounds fun. At bar w/ clients. Only place open in this storm.
Had a few too many. Love you.

That made me feel a little better. He wasn't alone in a hotel room eating bad room service. And if he was out drinking, I could have a harmless trip to a museum with two old friends, right?

By the time the three of us saw the first Hokusai print, I realized I had no reason to be nervous at all. Sylvia began going on and on about Hokusai, and she took over the entire conversation. In fact, she took over the entire room. She spoke so loudly and with such authority on the art that people thought she was a museum guide. They soon began to follow us from room to room.

At one point as Sylvia lectured everyone, I smiled up at Adam and shook my head. He bent down and whispered, "No, she hasn't changed."

After moving through a few rooms, she announced, "We'll now be entering an exhibit of ancient Chinese artifacts, primarily from the Shang Dynasty…"

Adam nodded to a bench. "Do you want to sit this one out?"

"Sure." As Sylvia led a group inside the next room, I sat down. "I love Asian art, but I've seen a lot before."

"How come?"

"When Logan was governor, we traveled a few times to Asia. You know, trade trips and stuff."

"It sounds like you've traveled a lot, then. You did when you lived in Mexico as well, right?"

"Oh yeah, I did a lot there, too — throughout Central America. And then with Logan, a little in Europe."

His brow furrowed slightly, and I knew I'd stepped in it. He surely wondered why I had gone to Europe and never contacted him. I quickly added, "But never to England. Only Berlin and Brussels."

He nodded as if he accepted my explanation. "The president is going to Berlin again next week for the summit."

"Hopefully I can get away for an hour. It has some great museums."

"That sounds like fun, and it would be nice for you — to get a break from the stress."

"Yeah, my job is stressful, no doubt about that, but it's also amazing and rewarding and can be a lot of fun." I smiled.

Just then Sylvia walked back into our room with her followers, who seemed to hang on her every word. She turned to them and said, "Well, thank you so much for joining me today. I really loved it. I should probably get back to my friends now."

Walking back over to us, she laughed. "Sorry about that. I should've warned you. It happens a lot. I just can't help sharing with people everything that I know."

"Can we get on with our own tour now?" Adam asked as he impatiently gripped his parka. Age really hadn't changed their interactions. He was still the bossy big brother, and she was still the annoying little sister.

We made our way through more of the gallery and then wandered over to the Freer. The Peacock room was especially gorgeous. The elaborate gold and blue designs really did remind me of a peacock's feathers, and the porcelain it housed was equally fine. It was the sort of room you wanted to stay in for a while and enjoy its uniqueness.

I asked, "Do you mind if we sit down for a minute here? It's beautiful, and I'm a little tired."

Sylvia checked her watch. "I don't really have time if I'm going to meet up with George to see that collection."

Maybe a little tired himself, Adam leaned against the wall. "What exactly are we seeing? I'd like to sit down for a few minutes as well."

"Oh, it's wonderful stuff that no one gets to see." Sylvia's eyes lit up. "Since the galleries are part of the Smithsonian, they're government-funded. There are pieces the museum has in its holdings but never displays because Americans are such prudes." She turned to me and said, "Your crazy right wing would go mad."

"So it's political art?" I asked.

"Oh no. It's *Shunga*. Japanese erotic art."

Erotic art? What the hell? There was no way I was going to look at porn with Adam. No way, no way. I glanced over at him, and he looked pissed. Did Sylvia think she was doing us a favor?

I tried to crack a joke, one that had some truth to it. "I'm sorry, Sylvia. It's nice of you to arrange it, but as you said, Americans are prudes, and I work at the White House. I'll stay here."

"Indeed," said Adam. "The deputy White House press secretary probably shouldn't be on a private tour of hidden erotica at the Smithsonian." He scowled at his sister. "I'll keep her company. You go ahead."

"Oh, you two have always been such duds." She chuckled and walked on. "I'll go by myself and meet you back here in half an hour or so."

As she huffed out of the room, I said, "I hope she's not upset."

"Who bloody cares? That's not something I want to see with my sister."

But would he have wanted to see it with me? I gave him a sly look before turning away.

"Let's sit down," I heard him say. I looked over, and he walked toward a bench.

Joining him there, I said, "It's such a beautiful room."

"My mum would love it. The next time they visit, I should bring them here."

"Are they coming soon?"

"Nothing is planned." His eyes moved around the room as if he were studying the people around us. Only two other visitors remained, and they headed toward the door — likely fleeing before the impending snowstorm outside would hit. Adam's expression became grim. "Actually, I don't know why I said that. They won't be coming again. There won't be any more plans. My dad is so ill that it's not possible."

"Oh, Adam. I'm sorry." My heart sank for him again. "How often are you able to see them?"

"I usually go home once a month. Sylvia does as well. I haven't been back in six weeks, though, so I'm taking time off after Berlin to see him."

"That must be very difficult." My grandmother had died of cancer, so I knew what it was like to watch someone's life come to a close over the course of visits. It was like reading a book that you hoped would get better with each chapter, but instead it got worse. Some stories never had a happy ending.

I tried to find something encouraging to say. "It's still nice that you can visit often—that you can see him even though you live in another country. I bet he really appreciates it."

"Well, my mum does." He laughed. "I guess he likes having us around. Sylvia talks his ear off. He and I don't talk much, so we end up watching a lot of football."

"But isn't that what men do?" I smiled. "Instead of talking about important things, they just talk about sports."

"Excuse me." He was playfully indignant. "Are you saying my father and I are insensitive?"

"Absolutely."

"And do you see your family often?" He seemed eager to change the subject away from himself.

"Some. They were both here for the inauguration. I usually see my dad a fair amount. President Logan's home is still in Chicago. And when I'm in California for work, I visit my mom. Last year with the campaign, my life was crazy and I was never home, so she didn't visit me, but she'll come to DC now that I'm here."

"What about Houston? Do you ever go back there?"

"Occasionally, to see friends and…" My speech halted altogether, and I stared at him. Once again in my life, I was about to tell Adam something about my sister I never told anyone. His gaze held mine as if he knew what might be coming. Had he set me up for it? Was he curious himself? Whatever the reason, as usual I *wanted* to tell him.

"When I'm there," I said, "I stop by my sister's grave."

"That's understandable. I would do the same thing. Besides, you grew up with her in Houston. It's home," he said delicately.

Whenever he treaded so lightly around my emotions, yet acknowledged them just the same, it just made me more comfortable expressing them. "But it's not home anymore." My lip shook, and the tears I normally suppressed tumbled forth. "I feel bad that we've all moved away."

His eyes went wide, like he was mortified he'd made me cry. "Nicki." He put his arm around me. "I'm sorry. I didn't mean to pry or make you sad."

"It's like we've left her behind," I gasped, recognizing my guilt for permanently abandoning Lauren to a friendless graveyard. The nook of his arm provided safe haven for feeling what I needed to, just as it always had, and I wanted to bawl my eyes out. But I couldn't. This time I was an adult in a public place. Even if no one was in the room with us, I shouldn't have been crying in the arms of another man than Juan Carlos, especially one who happened to also be a BBC reporter.

I pulled away and patted the tears off my cheeks. "I know it's silly, but if I have to fly through Houston, I'll even schedule a long layover just to go to the cemetery."

"That's nice, but your sister isn't there," he said, rubbing my back. "Not really. She's with you. In your heart. Right?"

Breathing deeply, I tried to pull myself together. "I know it makes no sense. Intellectually, I get it. Her soul is gone and elsewhere, but I hate that her remains are still there in that cemetery when none of us live near her." I let out a throaty laugh. "I always said we should have scattered her ashes in the Gulf. Then she'd be everywhere."

"It does appear to have its benefits." He grinned, probably happy I felt okay enough for a joke. He stopped rubbing my back but let his hand rest above my waist, and I didn't stop him. "Do you talk with your parents about it?"

Had he remembered so little about me? I'd turned to him when we were young in part because my mom had been so checked out and my dad lived over a thousand miles away. I gave him a skeptical look. "My dad brings Lauren up occasionally, but my mother…it's not really a welcome topic."

"Still?"

A smile escaped me. He *had* remembered. "Time has passed, and I may be older, but my mom still doesn't talk about the death of her little girl."

He sighed and stretched out his legs. "And probably never will."

"Nope."

Silence ensued, and I felt his hand hesitantly withdraw from my back. After a moment, he declared, "Tell me about where you've been to—like China. I've always wanted to go there, but I haven't yet had opportunity."

Good. We're out of the emotional danger zone, I thought, and I really didn't want to be a crying mess when Sylvia came back. I nodded. "China is an amazing country, but we were there talking trade. It's odd that they're Communists because they're such ardent capitalists."

"I know. They're Communists only when it comes to their authoritarian government. They couldn't care less about redistribution of wealth."

"Exactly, but it's still fascinating to be there, seeing modern China contrasted against its ancient history. The people were so friendly, and we were able to do some sightseeing. The Forbidden City is amazing, and I also went to the Great Wall."

"That's something I'd like to see."

"Yeah. I wanted to go there because it was something Lauren always wanted to do." *Ugh.* I'd done it again. I could not let Adam turn into my emotional sounding board. I had a boyfriend for that. With a quick pat of the bench to end the conversation, I immediately rose and said, "I need to find a ladies' room. I'll meet you back here."

After I pulled myself together in the bathroom, I stood in the hallway for a moment, scanning my emails and texts. I soon heard Sylvia's stiletto boots clack on the floor and looked up.

"Hello. I'm sorry you missed the display. It was amazing." She grinned.

"I'm sure," I said with a smile. The woman still didn't get that it was inappropriate for me on so many levels. Yet I sort of admired that she existed in her own little world where everything was simple and she was always right.

When we met back up with Adam, Sylvia said, "Should we go to the National Gallery now?"

Shaking my head, I pointed to my phone. "My conference call this evening was canceled because people are stuck in airports. It's dumping snow outside. If I'm going to get a cab home, I should go find one now."

"A taxi? Don't be silly," Sylvia said. "Adam can give you a lift, but really you should stay for dinner tonight if you're free. I'm cooking."

"Oh, that's nice of you to offer." I had no idea how to respond. I wanted to say yes, but should I? And did Adam even want me there?

"Please do," Adam said eagerly. "David's not there, so the place is actually clean for once."

"Oh…okay." I clenched my bag, hoping I made the right choice.

When we arrived at his car, snow covered it, so he told us to get in and get warm while he dusted it off.

"I'll sit in the back," said Sylvia happily. "I don't mind."

"Okay." I felt like we were replaying our roles from 1993.

Ever the gentleman, Adam opened the doors for us and shut us in. I huddled in my seat trying to get warm, though shivering had its benefit of releasing nervous energy. When he got in, he revved the engine for a second and then looked at me. It was déjà vu all over again. Adam and I together in the front seat of a car, only now the car wasn't his high school Honda. Now he drove a sleek BMW.

"Sorry about the cold leather. The seat warmer switch is on your left if you want it. The control for your side of the heat is on the dashboard."

"Thanks," I whispered, feeling another urge to text Juan Carlos. While Adam drove and talked with Sylvia, I whipped out my phone and dashed off a carefully crafted message.

Hi, sweetie. Having dinner with these two.
I'll call you later. I love you.

His reply soon popped up.

Still drinking. Hope I can even talk later. Love you, mi reina.

Somehow just checking in with Juan Carlos made me feel more at ease. I wasn't hiding anything, or at least not much.

When we got to Adam's apartment in Dupont Circle, we first took off our wet coats and boots. Standing in his apartment in my wool socks, I felt more comfortable as I looked around the large open space that flowed from the kitchen to a dining and living area.

"Your place is so nice," I said.

"That's because I designed it," said Sylvia.

"*You* picked out the art," Adam said as he hung up our coats. "*I* chose the furniture."

"What? We gutted the entire space, and I designed the layout and placed everything." She grabbed my hand. "Come on. I'll take you on a tour while Adam gets us some wine and starts a fire."

"Okay." I laughed nervously. "But, Adam, please don't go out of your way."

"Not at all. I was going to do it." His smiling eyes for me morphed into a glare for his sister. "I didn't need to be told."

Sylvia tossed her head and ignored him as she began to tell me about how she came up with the design. When she got to the mantle, she then went on about the painting she'd chosen to rest above it. I sipped the wine Adam had provided and stayed tuned in to Sylvia as best I could. After she finished, she announced, "Let me take you through the rest of the flat."

Oh God. Adam's bedroom? I didn't have time to object before she walked on, and I had to catch up with her. First she led me into the spare bedroom and its attached bath. Maybe if I knew more about decorating I would've been as impressed as she was with the Italian tile. When she led me out of the bedroom, I headed left to return to the living room. There was Adam standing in the hallway before me.

Sylvia headed in the other direction and asked, "We can go in your room, right, Adam?"

I met his gaze and really wanted to tell him he didn't have to let us, but that might have sounded even worse than saying nothing.

He simply said, "Sure."

He hadn't sounded incredibly enthused, but he followed us along. Now I was really nervous as I entered his room. The cream-colored space had a large bay window with two leather chairs in a sitting area, and beyond that was a large alcove that looked to be a little home office. A king-sized bed sat in the middle of the room.

Sylvia pointed to the art above the bed. "This is a very special print. The artist worked on it for months…"

She continued talking, but I stopped listening. Adam's bed was too much of a distraction. I let my eyes drop down to inspect the perfectly made blue duvet and matching shams. Adam's bed—where every night he slept and probably did all sorts of things with many different women. I didn't like thinking about the latter, so I wondered instead what he looked like sleeping in it. That made me crack a smile, which I had to hide.

After she finished with the art, Sylvia faced the rest of the room. "That alcove is a work area I designed. I like a more open space rather than a separate office. Now let's go back to the living room, and I'll cook."

She turned around, but I was intrigued by the artwork above his desk, which was really a drafting table. "You still draw?" I asked him.

"Yeah." He seemed sheepish.

"That's wonderful."

"I don't know." Running his hand through his hair, he said, "It's only a hobby."

"Can I see?" I didn't wait for an answer. I was too curious. Adam had drawn political cartoons and caricatures when we were young. I'd thought he was really good at the time and wondered what he did now.

From behind, I heard Sylvia say, "I'll be in the kitchen."

I picked up a sketch from his messy desk. "So you're doing caricatures of President Logan?"

"I'm trying," Adam said, walking up behind me.

"Can I see some more?"

"Of course." He pulled a stool out for me. "Take a seat."

As I studied all the drawings on the table, he sat on another stool beside me. His work had matured. The drawings were sharper, and the contexts were more informed. That made sense. He was a reporter now, after all.

I smiled. "These are so good, Adam. Why aren't you publishing them?"

"I don't think they're really good enough." He grimaced. "Plus, it's a hard profession to break into."

"But you're already a journalist. I would think it would be a leg-up. People know you. It should be easier to get them seen."

"I'm a television journalist. You know we're looked down upon by print. It probably hurts more than helps me that I'm already in the field."

I gently tapped a drawing. "I still think you should try. You'll never know if you don't, and wouldn't you rather be drawing than your current job?"

"Well, yes, but it seems like a futile endeavor. Not even worth the effort."

I wondered why he was so defeatist, but I didn't press him. Instead, I studied the work itself. I held up the drawing of President Logan. "You've really captured him well, but you could add something here. You're right that he's got a really long neck, but in this drawing—where he's angry—you should make some veins bulge out. They always do when he's pissed, though that's rare."

"Are you giving me secrets about your boss, Nicole Johnson?" He laughed.

"Hardly." I smiled. "He'd think these were hilarious. Now, he may not like the captions you put with them, but he'd like the drawings themselves and wouldn't mind them being accurate. He's got a really good sense of humor."

"Thanks. That's good to know."

"I like that one, too," I said, spying a cartoon of Gordon Brown. "He's probably a fun one to draw."

"Definitely. He's got a million different expressions, and he looks uncomfortable in every one of them." Sounding a little more confident, he pulled out a sketchpad and said, "This is what I'm working on right now. I thought I'd practice Angela Merkel since we're going to Berlin."

"Oh, let me see." I looked at the sketch. "This is really good. I've met her before. I'd give her a short necklace. She wears them all the time, even though they're not very flattering."

"What do you mean?"

"They show off her jowls."

"Let me add a necklace, then," he said, grabbing a pen.

As he sketched away, we talked about his drawings and the people in them. He wouldn't believe me when I told him they had potential, and I certainly didn't believe him when he said I was helping him. "How on earth am *I* helping *you?*"

"You have good insight." And then he gave me a compliment. "You're very clever, you know."

Years ago, he'd called me clever. It was the first compliment he had ever paid me, and I think I had blushed for a week after he'd said it. Today, normally somebody telling me I was smart was no big deal. It would go in one ear and out the other. Coming from Adam, though, it was an entirely different matter.

"Whatever," I said, but I felt a full-fledged flush come over me, starting with my cheeks and spreading all over. When I tried to look him in the eye, I noticed he wasn't looking at my face. His eyes wandered around my body, obviously checking me out. From his expression, I guessed he liked what he saw, but he was still polite and said nothing.

Out of the corner of my eye, I caught a glimpse of his bed—not what I needed to see at that moment. I looked down and said under my breath, "I should go see what Sylvia is up to."

"Of course." His lips twitched into a smile.

We walked back to the kitchen, and everything was normal again. Throughout dinner, Sylvia kept us laughing—sometimes at her, but usually with her—and her cooking, like her art and sense of style, was amazing.

After dinner, I checked my watch. "I really should get home," I said with some regret.

"When do you get to the office in the morning?" Sylvia asked. "Maybe we could meet for coffee."

"I don't think so." I chuckled. "Unless you want to meet me at six. I'm at my desk by seven."

Sylvia giggled. "Perhaps not, then." She pointed to the mess in the kitchen. "I hope you don't mind, but I'll let Adam take you home while I tidy up."

Alone in a car with Adam? Not just alone in a public museum? I took a deep breath. It shouldn't matter. And if it shouldn't matter, I had the power to make sure it didn't. I smiled at Sylvia. "Well, if Adam takes me home, then I have to say goodbye to you now."

With the snow falling heavily, there was plenty for Adam and me to talk about as we made our way to Lisa's apartment. We had a safely boring conversation about the strange weather for March and poor road conditions. That was helpful, as I needed to figure out how I was going to say goodbye.

Just as we pulled into the apartment building's circular driveway, I stole a look at him. Yes, he looked older than he used to, but in jeans, he resembled young Adam more. When he stopped the car, he turned to me with such a knowing smile that the words of my planned goodbye escaped me for a moment.

Instead, I contemplated what it might be like to kiss him again. Would it be the same? I could see my old friend Rachel laughing and saying, "Like Adam Kincaid forgot how to kiss? If anything, it's going to be even better." That got my mind in even more trouble.

After a day like we'd had together, I had the urge to say goodbye like when he used to drop me off. I wanted to climb into his lap, kiss him long and hard, and rub myself against his dick for so long we'd both be panting with want. At that moment, it seemed like such a good bad idea, and when he gave me that sly look, I was pretty sure he'd welcome whatever I did.

Then I remembered Juan Carlos, and a punch of guilt caused my prepared words to finally rush out of me. "Thanks so much for letting me crash your day with Sylvia, and thank you for dinner and the ride home."

"Well, you have to thank Sylvia for dinner, but the rest has been fun. I'm happy we got to spend some time together."

"I am, too," I said in a confessional whisper.

Our eyes locked, a little too long and a little too intensely, causing my thoughts to stray again. I had to stop wondering what it would be like to kiss him. There was no way I could be friends with the guy when my every instinct was to throw myself at him.

A smile slowly formed on Adam's face, and he said, "Now go on up. We've got a big week ahead, you especially."

I nodded. "The president's first international trip."

"Indeed."

After I made it inside the apartment, I peeked in the living room. Lisa had clearly spent the day sacked out on the couch. Huddled under a quilt, she had everything she needed within hand's reach — her phone, the remote, Diet Coke, takeout, and a glass of wine.

"Where have you been all day, stranger?"

"Out." I coyly studied the fringe on a throw pillow before I smiled. "With Sylvia and Adam. We had dinner at Adam's place together. Sylvia cooked."

"Ah ha." Her expression was full of judgment, but she said nothing else.

"I'm not hiding anything. Juan Carlos knows." Thank God I'd told him. Otherwise I would've backed down from her stare.

"Yeah…" After a second, she must've decided to keep her analysis of my private life to herself. She smirked. "I also sort of spent the day with the Kincaid family."

"What do you mean?"

"The cousin called me…more than once."

"I don't believe he's technically a Kincaid," I said with a giggle. "His mother is Adam's aunt."

"That's what he keeps telling me. He says his side of the family is much more down to earth than the Kincaids."

"How did he get your number?"

"Adam found it for him. The bastard." She smiled.

"Wow. He's persistent."

"Very."

"Would you go out with him?"

"I don't know..." she said. Her eyes narrowed at me. "Would you go out with Adam?"

The fringe on the pillow became fascinating to me as I mulled it over. If Juan Carlos weren't in the picture and I was honest with myself, the answer would be yes. At a minimum, I wanted to tear his clothes off and have my way with him one more time. I tried to find a genuine middle ground. "I was out with him today, but it wasn't a date. I think there's a difference." With more confidence, I added, "I have a professional stake in this, too."

Lisa pursed her lips in what had to be another round of judgment, but eventually she allowed a smile to creep through. "Well, I'd go out with David if it wasn't a date, so we're even."

Chapter Six

Air Force One was a giddy place the evening the plane took off for Berlin. Everyone, from the reporters to the staff to the president himself, was excited about the first international trip. Not that the groups really interacted much. The president had spacious private quarters, where he could do everything from work out to sleep to watch TV on a big flat screen, and then a large office upstairs. In the far back of the plane, the White House Press Corps traveled like they were in coach on any American airline. The president's staff was quartered in somewhat better accommodations toward the plane's front, and with a full office for us to work in.

My job had me making the rounds everywhere. As Matt walked alongside me, he yawned before giving me the job he didn't want to do. "Just tell them we'll give them extra time with the president later in the trip."

"Okay, but they're going to complain…"

"They're the press. All they do is bitch and moan." He waved his hand. "The quicker you tell them, the quicker you can catch some sleep."

As I walked down the stairs to the media, I heard a ruckus over the airplane engines. Rowdy reporters. It was a good thing they weren't near Logan. He was a light sleeper and mean as a bear when you woke him up.

When I walked through the curtains, I saw what caused so much noise. Reporters were grouped in clusters, gossiping and chatting.

Some played cards while another group drank beer and wine and occasionally erupted in fits of laughter and squeals. I spotted Adam on the outskirts, where a few stragglers read or tried to catch some sleep. His *The Economist* magazine was in his hand, but his Bose headphones hung around his neck like he'd just taken them off. The crowd must've been bothering him. I gave him a small wave, just as I had every day since our Sunday together. The wave was easier than talking, but still friendly enough.

When I approached the loudest group, I first saw Lydia Mixon in the center of it. She was the perky correspondent from CBS News, and she had to have been a cheerleader in high school, the kind Adam had once dated. If we were in high school, Lydia wouldn't have given me, the geeky outsider, the time of day. Now roles were reversed, and I was the one in power.

She caught my eye and grinned. "Hi, Nicole. It's good to see you. Are we being too loud?"

"No. No one has complained." I smiled at the group. "But you do seem to be having a good time? What's going on?"

"Just a little impromptu party." Lydia gestured to Dan Roark, who stood hunched over the back of a seat, holding a glass of beer. "Dan has us playing games that are making us laugh."

"Drinking games?" I asked Dan.

"Nah. More like truth or dare, but without the dare."

"Oh dear," I said in a playful tone.

Lydia sidled up to me and said, "Well, it's a little silly, but we're having fun."

"Dare I ask what 'truth' everyone is revealing?"

"We've been sharing where we lost our virginity and to whom," she said. "It's harmless."

I froze my smile. *Holy shit.*

Leaning closer to me, Dan asked, "Wanna play, Nicole?"

"Nah, I don't think so." I played it cool, hoping I could end it all sooner that way.

"I'll tell you mine," he said. "My high school girlfriend, Charlotte Clark, in my Mustang. How's that? Now your turn."

"Uh-uh." I shook my head.

"C'mon." Dan took a step toward me and pointed to Adam. "Even Kincaid played. Right, Kincaid?"

I turned to see Adam's response. I could've played the game for him. I knew whom he'd lost his virginity to and where. It wasn't me but his old girlfriend — the girl he'd cheated on me with. Adam's eyes met mine for a brief second, but they were blank. He silently waved his hand as if brushing it all aside.

Dan rolled his eyes. "So now he won't play. Whatever, Kincaid." He then turned to me. "Kincaid's girl was named Kate. They did it in his childhood bed. Now you tell us, Nicole."

I knew Adam and Dan didn't like each other. If Dan's reporter sixth sense had picked up on something in Adam's past to exploit, I was sure the comment had been a dig at Adam, not me. But now I was the collateral damage, and it was worse than a blow to the gut. It was a rapid-fire machine gun, leaving multiple and increasingly severe wounds.

"Kincaid's girl" — a girl other than me. "Kate" — the name I'd hated for years. "They did it" — yes, they had, many times. And finally, the worst part — "in his childhood bed" — their history and family connection was part of what had driven Adam to her after I'd rejected him.

As nauseated as I was at hearing about Kate and Adam having sex and then my name being thrown in, I was sure Adam was even less comfortable at that moment. In the end, he'd been hurt just as much as me, both today and back then. I even felt a little sorry for him.

I heard Lydia say, "Please, Nicole. It's not like we know the guy. It's just for fun."

I bet Adam was truly mortified by that one, and it actually made me crack a smile. I decided to give them a tidbit. "At the beach," I said curtly.

"How sweet," said Lydia. Other female reporters chimed in with "sexy" and "romantic."

But the tidbit wasn't enough for Dan. It only egged him on. "So how was it? Were you in high school? Was it any good?"

"No more information."

"Come on, Johnson," he said. "'At the beach' tells us almost nothing. We're reporters. You know you've got to give us something more than that."

I shook my head, mainly at myself. I shouldn't have ever opened up the topic; it was my own fault. "Fine," I said, crossing my arms. "I was seventeen. It was Valentine's Day. That's all —"

"Were you in love?" asked Lydia.

I could've balked at the question, but I didn't. Answering it felt as easy as saying the sky was blue. "Yes." In my next breath, I went back to my job. "Now that I've disclosed that bit of personal information, maybe you won't be too upset when I tell you the president won't take formal questions from the media until the joint press conference tomorrow."

The reporters around me groaned and griped, but I continued smiling. "Don't worry. You'll have more opportunities. Thanks, y'all," I said, retreating to my seat that was far away, but not far enough. I wanted to retreat from the world.

When I walked by Matt, he called out, "Get some sleep, okay, Nicole? You're going to need it."

I nodded. *Gladly.* Following orders, I grabbed my sleep mask from my bag. I'd look like Holly Golightly, but it was worth it for the darkness.

As I bedded down in my seat with a blanket and pillow, the mask gave me a sense of privacy. I nestled into my pillow, and that day at the beach came back to me. No matter what, I always felt blessed I had been in love with my first...

Adam rolled on his back, and after a few seconds of silence, he talked to the sky. "I want to be with you, Nicki. I want to be your first. I know it's silly and stupid, but it would mean so much to me."

When I didn't immediately respond, he looked over at me. "But I understand if you don't. If you want to wait...for someone who will be sticking around."

Sticking around? Why would I want to wait for that guy—if that guy even ever came around? I only wanted Adam. I smiled to put him at ease. "I want it to be you. Now."

"Now?"

"Now."

He looked back and forth at our open surroundings. "But we're outside, and you'll get cold."

"I don't care, and no one is around. We're in the middle of nowhere."

Making sure he had his wallet, he guiltily remarked, "I have something..."

I got excited to tell him my surprise. "We don't need it. I'm on the pill."

"You are?"

"Yeah, for a while now."

*The prospect of condomless sex must've startled him. "I've never…
done that before."*

"Well, then you'll have a first, too."

Three days later, we'd finished our final scheduled event for the summit. Logan scheduled some down time to rest before we moved on to Nigeria. Work demanded I prepare for that next leg of the trip, and the bed at my hotel called me to sleep, but how often was I ever in Berlin?

Deciding I'd work on the plane later that day, I planned to sneak away for a few hours. As I walked to the subway, it felt like playing hooky, though it was less fun doing it alone. But I couldn't ask anyone from work to join me; I didn't want it to get out I was slacking.

And then Adam popped into my mind. He'd said it would be fun to see a museum in Berlin, and I was heading to one. It would be just a short run through a gallery, not a date or anything. Juan Carlos wouldn't care, and professionally, it was on the up and up. I told myself I could be mature. I could look but not touch — and no crying on Adam's shoulder this time.

So I texted him.

> *Hi. It's Nicki. Any interest in catching a museum with me?
> I'll be at the Museum Berggruen at 3. It's across from the
> Charlottenberg Palace. I understand if you can't.*

It took a moment for him to respond, but when he did, I smiled.

> *See you at 3. Cheers.*

When he met me at the museum, I was so engrossed with my phone, he surprised me as I heard him say, "Hello, Nicki."

"What? Oh. Sorry. I was just sending something." I saw he'd changed into jeans, but he still wore his starched white dress shirt from the press event that morning. The combination was sexy beyond belief. "Thanks for coming. I know it's out of the way, but Sylvia told me it's a great collection. Not many people come out here." That was one of the reasons I felt safe meeting him there.

"Thanks for inviting me," he said with a grin.

"Sure." I nodded toward the door. "Let's go in."

The collection of Picasso, Klee, and Matisse was impressive, though I thought Sylvia would've enjoyed it more than us. We blew through it in half an hour. As we stood awkwardly on the museum steps, Adam said, "Do you want to go sit for a while? Maybe in the park?"

"Sure." Sitting in a park was a platonic thing to do, though I touched my throat as if I needed another alibi. "Actually, I'm a little thirsty."

"Let me get you something."

He ran over to a street seller and bought a couple of bottles of Orangina, and we found a spot on a bench in front of the stately palace. I thanked him again for the drink, and he said, "It's the least I can do. Thank *you* for inviting me today. It was very interesting. I haven't seen that many Picassos except in the museum in Paris."

"Same with me."

"When were you in Paris last? With Logan?"

"No. New Year's." I took a sip and admitted, "With Juan Carlos."

"New Year's in Paris. Nice." He stretched his legs out and gave me a skeptical look. "So tell me about Juan Carlos."

I leaned back a bit in disbelief. "You really want to talk about him?"

"Sure. He's important to you, right?"

"Of course." But telling an old boyfriend about a new boyfriend—and vice-versa—was always something I avoided.

"Then get on with it."

"Well…you probably know a lot. His family was part of the Mariel Boatlift from Cuba when he was a boy. They came here with nothing and became prosperous. He's been in politics for forever. He—"

"No. Tell me about him."

"Um, what do you want to know?"

"We're friends. You can tell me. What do you like about *him?*"

Wow. Adam had just said we were friends, but that question seemed beyond ex-lovers-turned-friends. There was no way in hell I ever wanted to hear why he was drawn to Felicity. I was too jealous to be that good of a friend, but he obviously felt differently. He wasn't jealous and wanted to be my buddy. I wasn't sure I was ready for that.

"What do I like about *him?*" I asked.

"Yes."

"Well…he's very charismatic, very personable. People just want to be around him."

"That's often said."

"It's true, though. He's not a very big guy, but he's got a giant personality. He's very endearing."

"What else?"

"Well, we care about the same things. You know, have the same politics."

"And?"

"And he's a very passionate person. He couldn't be as dedicated to his work without that drive. It's one of the things we have most in common."

"What do you mean?"

"Well, I work long hours. I miss a lot of personal stuff in life. Most guys don't understand that—even some political types don't get it."

"You do need someone understanding of that."

"I love his family, too." I smiled, thinking of his wonderfully kind folks. "It's big and friendly. Even though I'm not Cuban, they've been incredibly welcoming to me. I suppose knowing Spanish helped with that. His mom is great, and his father kind of dotes on me. He calls me *Blanquita*—like I'm Snow White because I'm so pale. It's really sweet."

"A big family is nice," he said, looking away for a moment.

"It is." I grimaced. "Sometimes I feel very alone. It feels good to be around them."

"Do you want a big family?"

"Yeah. Actually, I do. Not too big, but I'd like to have three kids." I took a steadying breath. "After Lauren died, I was by myself. I was the only child, and my sister—my friend—was gone, and I felt a lot of responsibility for my parents. I think with three kids, if something happens to one of them, you still have someone."

He nodded and smiled. "I feel lucky to have David. He's like a brother to me and Sylvia."

"I don't know, though." I sighed. "I turn thirty-four this year, and I don't see kids on the horizon anytime soon." I eyed him. "What about you? Do you want to have kids?"

"Well, of course. I'd love a family."

For a second I wondered what Adam's idea of a family was, and my heart sank. His planned family no doubt included a gorgeous, proper British wife like Felicity and two towheaded children in little prep school uniforms. The very thought made me happy to have Juan Carlos.

Lost in my own ruminations, I rambled aloud, "Yeah, Juan Carlos is a really, really good guy, and he's good to me. And he's incredibly loyal. I mean…he works in politics…he's got pretty interns flirting with him all the time, but I trust him completely."

When Adam didn't say anything, my whole body tensed as I realized I'd made a colossal gaffe. I looked up at him and saw his sad frown. "Oh, Adam. I wasn't bringing that up…I didn't mean anything by it."

He shifted in his seat to face me, his expression pleading. "Nicki, you have to know how sorry I was…how sorry I am. I've carried guilt and regret with me for the last—"

"No. Don't say that. I have my own guilt…my own regrets—so many." I shook my head in a panic. "God. Please, let's not talk about it. It was years ago. It's not a big deal."

"Nicki, I want to talk, even if we're just going to be—"

"No. It's not necessary. We don't have to go there. I'm so sorry." I crossed my arms. "Let's let the past be the past and focus on the present."

"Okay." But he didn't sound okay. He looked at his watch, and I was sure that I'd somehow hurt him when he said, "I'm sorry, Nicki, but I've got to run. I've got a plane to catch."

"Oh. That's right. You're going to see your dad."

"Just for a few days."

"Will you tell your mom hello for me?" I smiled. "And your dad."

"Certainly. I know they'll be happy to hear from you. They watch you on the news."

"That's nice of them. Yet so…odd. Do you know what I mean?"

"I know exactly what you mean."

I played with the cap on my bottle as I considered this understanding we seemed to share. We had both a history and a sense of what it all meant in the present; plus, we saw each other at work every day. There were multiple connections between us. We were tied to one another whether I wanted to be his friend or not.

I noticed he checked his watch, and I sighed. "I suppose I need to leave, too. We're off to Nigeria tomorrow."

"I'll be back in DC by the time you arrive in the States on Sunday."

"Maybe we can talk again then," I ventured.

"I'd like that," he said with a smile that somehow set me at ease. "I'd like that very much."

Chapter Seven

When I left Adam in Berlin, I said we'd talk again in a few days, but by the evening of the following day, I was antsy. A few days seemed too long to wait. Maybe he was right. We could be friends, even if I was a little jealous of his girlfriend and wanted to jump his bones. I was an adult. I could get over those things, right?

I wondered if Felicity was with him in Cambridge. Were they close enough that she would visit his gravely ill father? I was dying to know. Yet whether it was for professional reasons or because of his girlfriend, I knew Adam wouldn't call me. If I wanted to talk to him before bumping into each other in the White House briefing room with a hundred reporters listening, I would have to call him.

That night, I sat in my hotel room with nothing to do but more work or watching TV. I stared at the phone, thinking Nigeria was only an hour ahead of London time. Should I just touch base with him?

For my job, I was constantly thinking up narratives that would give a positive context to the president's actions. Some people called it spin, but spin was usually something we did as damage control. A narrative was an offensive strategy where we shaped the story before it got out.

So what was my narrative for talking to Adam? I slowly nodded as my story started to take shape. An old friend was visiting his dying father—the thoughtful thing to do was check in and make sure things were okay. I wrinkled my nose. It barely passed the smell test, but it was good enough, and I reached for the phone.

"Hi, Adam," I said after he answered. "I hope I'm not calling too late."

"Not at all. It's good to hear from you."

"I'm sorry it's so late. It was a long day, but I wanted to see how you're doing."

"I'm fine. How are you?"

"Oh, you know." I chuckled. "You've probably read what I was working on today."

"Indeed, I have. Logan has received great press."

"It's been an amazing day. Nigeria is fascinating, and the visit has gone really smoothly so far. There's a great American grad student helping us with logistics. She's here doing research for her dissertation on the Nigerian government. Her name is Funmbi. She's a big fan of yours, by the way. She asked me if you were traveling with us."

"Is that why you're calling me?" He laughed, but he really did sound perplexed.

"If I spent my time informing you about all your legions of female fans, I wouldn't be able to get my work done."

"Rubbish."

"I just wanted to make sure you were okay."

"Why wouldn't I be okay?" He hurriedly added, "Don't misunderstand me. I'm happy that you called."

"I know what it's like to be with someone who's really sick. You may not know this, but I went and lived with my grandmother when she had cancer…before she died." I started to speak in a rush. "So when you told me you were seeing your dad, I was worried about you." I completely garbled the last part in fear that Felicity was sitting happily at his side.

"That's nice of you. It has been a rough day."

"I'm so sorry." I hesitated for a second and asked, "Is Felicity there?"

"Er. No. Why do you ask?"

Thank God I got paid to think and talk on my feet. Otherwise I might have told him the truth — *"Because I'm insanely jealous of her."* Instead, I lied. "I was just wondering. I thought she might be able to help."

"No. She's in London working. I'll see her before I leave."

I liked the first part; I didn't like the latter. I tried to sound chipper. "So tell me what's going on."

"We visited my dad's oncologist this morning."

"How did that go?"

"Frankly, I should've known the news would be bad. Dad was trying so hard, though. Normally, he uses a walker, but he put up a front for me and used a walking stick."

"Could he still get around that way?"

"He took my arm, which helped."

"I bet he's really happy to have you there."

"I suppose."

"What did the doctor say?"

"That the cancer had become more aggressive." He sounded more bitter and resigned than sad.

"I'm so sorry. That must've put a terrible damper on the day."

"It's okay." He sighed. "It's an interesting dynamic in the house. Everyone speaks about the cancer like it's a minor illness and the doctors are just trying to get the prescription right when, in fact, it's fatal."

"I think that's the easiest way to manage the pain of seeing someone so ill. You get lost in the details."

"'Lost in the details.'" A bed creaked through the phone. He must've lain down as he said, "That's exactly what's going on. Meanwhile my father is literally shrinking before my eyes, and the house smells like a dodgy hospital."

"Oh, that smell! I know that smell."

"The smell sucks." He laughed.

"Where do you think it comes from?"

"I don't bloody know." His voice became a little mischievous. "I think the nurses bring it into the house."

"No, they're nice. They wouldn't do that."

"Then what's the cause? Because I'm fucking sick of it."

"I don't know…" Then I did a double-take at what he'd said. "Wow. You just said 'fuck.' I was beginning to think you'd given up cursing. You used to swear like a sailor when we were in high school, but not anymore."

"Give up cursing? You've got to be fucking kidding me. I curse all the bloody time."

"Not around me."

"That's because I've been trying to be good around the deputy White House press secretary."

"You're so full of it." I laughed, though I wondered if there was something to what he'd said.

"It's true."

"Oh yeah? Do tell."

"Fuck no," he said with snicker.

For the next few hours, we laughed and talked, and while it wasn't just like old times, it was a lot of fun. There were moments when it was better than our past, simply because I thought he was even more interesting now, but there was still our underlying relationship from our youth. Our past together just made the conversation richer. I watched the clock tick the hours away, not wanting to be the one who cut off the conversation.

Late in the night, he finally said, "Nicki, I'm so sorry. I've been talking your ear off, and I didn't notice the time. It's two in the morning." He then added, "You probably want to call Juan Carlos."

"No. I already talked to him earlier today. He's on a cross-country flight tonight." Mention of Juan Carlos was a reminder of my responsibilities, though. Reluctantly, I said, "But I should go to sleep. I'm not getting much of it these days."

"Well, thank you for calling…and listening. I really appreciate it."

"Don't thank me. I wanted to."

"I suppose I'll talk to you in a few days when we're back in DC."

My response was swift with no forethought or caution, just my own personal want. "No, I'll check in with you tomorrow. Night, Adam."

And I did—every night for the next three nights. His dad's health and family took up a chunk of every long call, but with each evening we talked more about other things: our work, our old friends, and what was going on in the world. Yet we never talked about what might be going on—or had gone on—between us. Instead, we chatted and laughed and teased one another.

The final night that we spoke, I couldn't stifle all my yawns as the clock ticked on. Adam said, "It's quite late, Nicki. You need to get to bed."

"It's okay. I'm in bed."

"Are you now?"

"Of course. It's after three."

"You're in bed. Now, that's something I'd like to see…again."

I had been in a half-dreamy state, but that woke me up. It was an unmistakable flirt, making me as flustered as a seventeen-year-old. "Uh…it's not very exciting. I'm staying at the Lagos Sheraton. I might as well be in Phoenix."

"What are you wearing?"

"A T-shirt." I gulped. I'd had enough phone sex with Juan Carlos to know what was coming next.

"Anything else?" he asked.

I shook my head. As much as I wanted to, I just couldn't go there. "Adam…"

"You can't blame me for trying."

I winced. What had I done? I'd started this, and maybe he thought I wanted a fling to remind us of old times. But as I pinched my brow with worry, he stunned me. "Nicki…you must know by now how much you mean to me. I adore you. I always have."

My hand searched my chest for my heart. Adam had crossed the line. The professionalism and friendship we'd so carefully established had been breached. And as worrying as that was, I was tickled to my core that our feelings from so long ago were reciprocal once again. Yet now I was mature enough to control them.

I couldn't say anything like that to him, though, even if it was truer than true. I stumbled. "And you mean…the world to me, Adam, but I don't know if…and then there's…" Defeated by all the complications between us, I sighed. "We should probably have this conversation in person."

"Probably so."

He sounded a little dejected, so I wanted to say something encouraging. "I want you to know our talks have been the highlight of my trip."

"Mine, too."

"I should go now. Good night. Have a safe trip back home."

"I'd tell you to have a safe trip as well, but I think Air Force One is pretty secure."

"That's true. It's the only time I'm not scared at all to be on a plane."

"Well, go get some sleep…in your T-shirt and what little else you're wearing." His swagger was back.

"Adam…" I giggled.

"Oh, don't mind me." He laughed. "Good night. We can talk next week."

Did things change between Adam and me because of that night, or had it been a slippery slope over time? Or, if I looked back on it, had anything ever changed?

Air Force One was the worst place to collect my thoughts on the matter, but it was also an in-my-face reminder of my problems. Work was all around me, people mentioned the BBC wasn't on the plane because Adam was with his dying father, and there was always the random friend of Juan Carlos's asking me to say hello.

Maybe it was my discomfort with the situation that made me rationalize my dilemma. Pretending to read a document on my laptop, I sat quietly in my seat and dissected my life. First, I set aside that I was supposed to be in a happy relationship with Juan Carlos. That was an issue unto itself. Then, I played out the problem with Adam. If anything happened between him and me and it got out, which it always did, it would disgrace us both professionally. In public relations, there was only one repeatedly proven method to weather a scandal — get all the bad information out there yourself as soon as possible. Full disclosure and nothing less.

It took me a nanosecond to reject that idea. Nothing had really happened between us yet. We'd simply expressed there was mutual interest. The timing wasn't ripe to disclose anything to our bosses or even our partners. What if nothing came of it? We could cause an unnecessary disaster for everyone.

But what of Juan Carlos? Was it just Adam who could turn my head, or could another guy do it as well? I didn't know. I was sure, though, that Juan Carlos and I couldn't move in together, at least not yet. With our travel schedules, things had already felt a little distant between us for a few weeks. Even the phone sex was non-existent because of the eight-hour time difference. Yet despite my feelings for Adam, I missed Juan Carlos. Maybe because I knew he would be there for me. Adam was still an unknown.

The middle of the following week, Lisa caught me before I left work for the day. "Where's Juan Carlos this weekend?"

"Hmpf," I grunted as I put in an earring. "He's here on Friday but leaves Saturday morning for Hawaii, of all places. There's a senate race."

"So you would be okay if I invited Adam and David over on Saturday night?"

My mouth gaped open. "What the hell? Are you kidding me?"

"Nope."

"What's changed?"

"It started when David sent me a dozen roses at work while you were gone."

"Really? So he asked you out properly?"

"Hardly." She shook her head. "He told me he wanted to play doctor."

"And you fell for that?"

"No way. I told him to knock it off."

"What did he say?"

"He asked if he could make it up to me by cooking dinner."

"And you said yes?"

"I said I'd only do it if you were there, too. He said three's a crowd but then asked if Adam could come, too."

"Does Adam know?"

"I'm not sure." She leaned against the doorjamb and eyed me. "So should I invite them over?"

What a little shit. She was forcing me to make the call for everyone. I would be the one to decide if things could proceed or not for either of us, and Adam would most definitely find out. I hadn't told her about our phone calls while we were away. If she knew that, I bet she'd demand I inform Juan Carlos immediately. Yet here she was practically setting me up to cheat on him. What was her deal?

"What's going on?" I casually put my other earring in. "Why are you doing this to me?"

"It looks to me like you need some help sorting your shit out. This is just a nudge."

"Okay, maybe I do…" I smiled. "What about poor David?"

"Did you just say 'poor David'?"

"Yeah."

"Pfft. As for 'poor David,' I'm just toying with him." She crossed her arms. "What's your answer?"

"Sure. It's just a dinner among old friends," I said, convincing no one.

"Very nice." She turned to walk away. "Good spin."

"Because it's the truth!" I called back.

The following day after the press briefing, Adam walked up to me with a smile. I'd just been grilled over health care, so he was a welcome sight.

"Morning, Adam," I said.

"Hello. It sounds like you've got your work cut out for you on the health care legislation."

"Yeah…well, any reform we do will be compared to the British system. That's both good and bad, as I understand it."

"Anything free at the point of access has to be good."

"Excellent point. I'll remember that." I grinned.

"Did I just give you a talking point?"

"Maybe." I scanned the room to see if anyone was in earshot before I asked in a low voice, "So, dinner with David and Lisa?"

"Odd…but I'm looking forward to it."

I studied his happy face. "I agree." I then gestured toward the door. "I've got a meeting. I'll see you tomorrow."

"Wait. Please. I've got a question."

"What's that?"

"Are you going to tell Juan Carlos?" he asked quietly, staring me down.

Dear God. That was a tougher question than anything I'd been hit with that morning on health care. My smile became firm. "No. There's nothing to tell. We're having dinner with friends. Have you told Felicity?"

"No, nor do I plan to."

"Because?"

"That could unnecessarily cock up everything."

"It could." I checked my watch to hide my glee that Felicity was being kept in the dark about me. "I'm late," I said as I looked up. "We can talk this weekend."

He smiled. "Yes, we can."

Chapter Eight

On Saturday night, I slowly slid the serrated knife through each tomato. I was too nervous to chop quickly. I'd probably slice off a finger, lose a ton of blood, and end up with an ambulance at our apartment building. Then there would be a whole lot of nosy neighbors, who all worked in or around the government, now curious why the BBC White House correspondent was at the deputy White House press secretary's apartment.

As I diced the tomatoes, I heard Lisa welcome Adam and David into the apartment. I could make out bits of conversation. There was talk of the size of the apartment, and it sounded like David had brought her flowers.

When they walked into the kitchen, the flowers entered the room first. "What a beautiful bouquet," I said and reached out to touch the giant arrangement.

"Not as pretty as the ladies tonight," said David. He swooped down and gave me a peck on the cheek. "How are you, Nicki dear?"

"Great," I said, sniffing his cologne. He smelled divine and looked even better. This would be a true test of Lisa's will. I grinned at the thought. "Thanks for coming."

Adam stood behind him, holding a bag of groceries. He appeared a little annoyed at David, but smiled at me. "Evening, Nicki. You do know you didn't have to cook."

"Oh, we just thought a salad might be nice," I said cheerily.

He wore a starched shirt, jeans that hung just so on his hips, and casual loafers. He looked every bit the dashing Brit. With a wink, he asked, "Just in case dinner was crap?"

"Maybe…" I smiled. "No, I'm sure David is a great cook."

"Let me show you what's for dinner," David said, taking the bag from Adam. He began displaying the contents on the worktop. "I'm making a traditional British meal—bangers and mash and spotted dick."

Oh God. I'd had spotted dick once in my life, served to me as a dessert by Adam's dear mum. The memory had stuck with me—there she was, in her kitchen drying her hands and saying, *"It's nice to see you again, Nicki. Maybe you want to sample some of the famous Kincaid spotted dick?"* I had been mortified because I'd had no idea what she was talking about. All I'd known was that my boyfriend's mom had said something about a Kincaid dick with freckles.

Smirking at the recollection, I glanced at Adam, who held up his hands in surrender. "I've had nothing to do with the planning of this meal."

"You're a reporter." I laughed. "You know ignorance isn't a very good defense."

Lisa chuckled as she examined the package of sausages and the can of spotted dick. "I detect a theme here."

"That's nice to hear, treacle," David said, putting his arm around her. "I was worried you might not pick up on it."

She snuck out from under his arm and handed him the bag of potatoes. "You should start peeling if we're going to eat before midnight. I'll get the water on."

While David and Adam peeled potatoes, I finished the salad, and Lisa kept the conversation going. Her work at NIH was interesting, and both David and Adam peppered her with questions. After a while, David leaned over her shoulder and murmured, "Such a big brain in such a pretty little head. We could have beautiful children."

"Yeah, right," Lisa said, jabbing her elbow into his side. "Speaking of children, Nicki, you missed a call from Rachel while you were at the grocery store. She's pregnant again."

"Oh my God," I said with a chuckle. "That will be three in five years. Congratulations to her, but wow. She's going to have her hands full. I'll call her tomorrow."

"It's nice to hear she's doing well," said Adam. "What's her husband like?"

"Local sportscaster," I said. "He's hilarious and dotes on Rachel. We like him."

Lisa poked David in the side. "*You* remember Rachel, *don't you?*"

"Hmm. Maybe." He smiled, shrugging it off. "Like I told you. Ancient history, love."

Surprisingly, David's dinner turned out just fine — except for the dessert. Lisa pushed her plate toward him. "I'm not very hungry any more. You can have mine."

"You don't like spotted dick from a tin?" David guffawed.

I took a bite and choked the nasty substance down my throat. "Um, Adam, I think I remember your mother's being better."

"My mum's is much better," he said as he poked the wet, spongy mass on his plate.

As we cleared the dishes, I wondered what might happen next. Earlier in the day when we'd discussed the evening, Lisa had suggested a movie. I offered Monopoly, thinking it was more platonic, but she never said yes or no, and I soon found out why. She barred Adam and me from entering the kitchen. "I can't clean with everyone in here. Nicki, you and Adam go out on the balcony. It's a nice night."

"Yeah. I guess so." I side-eyed her. This must've been a part of her plan to force me to address things with him. For that, I needed a drink. "Let's get another glass of wine."

When we stepped out onto the balcony, Adam sat down in one of the chairs while I walked to the railing. It was a warm April night, and the balcony was spacious with a beautiful view of the city. In the distance, you could see the Washington Monument rise through the black sky.

With Adam behind me and the darkness all around, I felt a little more confident. *What the hell,* I thought. *I might as well start from the beginning.* "I was sick the morning of that first press briefing, when we first saw each other again."

"You were ill? I'm sorry."

"Not that kind of sick. I was nauseated because I was nervous."

"It was an important day — the start of a new Presidency."

"It wasn't just that, though it certainly was a big day. But I've had big days in the past. I don't mind the spotlight." I turned around and leaned against the railing, though I still didn't look at him. "It was you. I couldn't believe you were going to be there."

"When did you hear?"

I slowly raised my head to see him warily studying me, as if he didn't know where the conversation was headed. I crossed my arms. "Juan Carlos and I had just gotten back from our vacation in Paris when I heard you'd taken the White House correspondent job. I got nervous immediately. Then, as it sunk in that I'd be seeing you every day, I was…well, Juan Carlos said I'd become 'distracted.' That's what he called it. I blamed it on my job."

"Distracted?" He smiled. "I'd say I've been distracted myself."

"I suppose it's good to know I'm not the only one." I snickered. "But that morning was bad."

"You didn't seem nervous at all."

"Oh, of course not. Over the years, I've become pretty good at putting up a front."

"I certainly can't argue with that. I'd say you're an expert."

Ouch. That was a dig, though I couldn't deny it was true. "Yeah, well…Anyway, when you came up to me to talk that day, I just couldn't do it. I didn't know why you were there—what you wanted. It was a shock just seeing you, and I needed to focus on work. That's why I walked away."

"I doubt I would've had very many good answers to your questions. It wasn't a rational move for me to have taken the job."

That made me frown. I felt like I'd actually revealed a little about myself, but Adam gave me nothing in return. "They're probably done cleaning," I said bitterly. "Let's go back inside."

Adam jumped up at once and came toward me. "No, Nicki. Let me explain. I *was* happy to see you that day. I'd been curious about you for years. And you looked the same…exactly the same. Just as beautiful as ever, but now you were this brilliant adult woman. After seeing you that morning, I knew I'd done the right thing. It was nice just to be near you again."

My hard heart softened to mush, and I smiled. "I felt the same way."

He leaned against the railing, and after he looked down at me, I could swear a kiss was on the horizon.

But there was still too much to say. I turned my head. "It just made things worse, though."

"Why?"

There I was with a brilliant reporter, and after months of going over the story of our lives, I'd buried the lead. It was time to bring it out into the open. "Juan Carlos has asked me to marry him."

Deep creases formed in Adam's brow, and his mouth opened and shut. I'd left him speechless and probably more irritated than sad.

"It was last year," I explained, not wanting him to hate me. "We'd only been together a few months, but he's a stereotypical Latin romantic. He said he knew from the beginning. Unfortunately, I was the opposite. I'm never sure about things like that. I'm always waiting for the other shoe to drop. I told him I needed time."

"What about living together? Are you still going to do that?"

"That was the compromise I made late last year. I mean…" I glanced back into the night as if the answers to my life's dilemma existed out there. "I do love him. He's a wonderful man, and he's been very persistent. Any woman would be crazy not to be with him."

"So why haven't you found a place?"

"That's Juan Carlos's question." I swallowed hard. "And he's right to ask it. It's been my fault. I could've picked an apartment—there are many, but I haven't."

"He's going to live there, too. Why didn't he find it?" He sneered. "I'd say you have the more important job by far."

"Yeah, well…there may be a little machismo there," I muttered. "I think the bigger issue is that the more I see you at work, the more distracted I've been with him."

"I've had the same experience with Felicity."

I didn't like hearing her name, though what he said was a little heartening. I thought of the round of perfunctory sex I'd had with Juan Carlos the night before and sighed. "I don't know what to do. Even if you're waltzing back into my life just to waltz right back out again, the fact is, I don't feel for Juan Carlos like I should."

"I don't really waltz," Adam said in a sour voice.

"I'm sorry. You get what I mean, though, right?"

"Sort of. What do you mean 'like you should'? How *should* you feel about Juan Carlos?"

Boy, he was just dragging this stuff out of me. Holding his gaze, I spoke from my heart. "Well, I've been with people…I've had relationships, but they've never felt like what we had together all those years ago. It could just be because we were so young and it was such an intense, short period of time, and maybe I'm romanticizing it. But I'd like it if some part of that feeling—that intensity—was there in a relationship with someone else."

His head inched closer to mine as I finished my sentence, and soon his lips were near mine, whispering, "Nicki, you still feel right to me."

I whimpered, not knowing what in the hell to do. "Oh God, no." I whirled around from him, only to spin back to face him. "I'm sorry. I shouldn't…I don't mean…"

He blinked repeatedly and sputtered, "I…uh…"

Adam Kincaid wasn't used to being denied a kiss. I wanted to laugh, but it was more important to explain myself. "No, I need to finish. Please, I need to tell you more."

"Right. Okay." He calmly leaned against the rail and crossed his arms in anticipation. "It's all right. I'm listening. So you and Juan Carlos—what's your 'status,' so to speak?"

"We're still seeing each other. He's my date for the White House Correspondents' Dinner. What about you and Felicity?"

"The same." He arched a brow like he'd lobbed the ball back to me.

"I don't want to do anything drastic, but I hate this hellish limbo."

"Why are you in limbo? And why is it hellish?"

"Why?" I gasped in exasperation. "Why? Because *you're* here! Because I've got a loving boyfriend I *was* thinking of marrying, and now that you're here I don't know what to think. I've got a job that I love, but if I were acting ethically, I wouldn't be standing here with you right now. I can hardly resign, though, because I've no idea what's going to happen with you. I don't want to throw this all away just to relive some good times for a couple of months."

Describing it aloud made the whole stupid mess seem like a joke. I smiled as I went over to the table and took a drink of wine before easing myself into a chair. "I could go to Logan tomorrow and say, 'Mr. President, you've known me a long time. You know I wouldn't do this lightly, but I've got a little problem. You're busy fighting terrorism and fixing the American economy, but I need to be reassigned somewhere in the bowels of government so I can hook up with my high school boyfriend, Adam Kincaid of the BBC.'"

"Well now, you wouldn't actually be talking to the president about this, would you?" Taking the seat beside me, he said, "You'd talk with Matthew. He's your boss, right? What would he say?"

"Oh yes, I would talk to Logan. I'd tell Matthew, too, but I'd go directly to Logan first. I owe him that. He's like my dad—not to mention friends with him. Logan would ask a lot of questions, and I'm not sure how it would go from there. I'd be a little political liability that needed to be fixed. They'd probably tell me to quit, or they'd reassign me to some crap job."

I shook my head. "But then, say, six months later, things end between you and me…for whatever reason. I can't go back to my old job—not to mention it would be a while before I get another decent one as a press secretary. I'd have a reputation for sleeping with the press. That would be horrible."

"Sleeping with the press—like me?" He gave me a sexy grin. "That would definitely be *horrible*."

"Horrible." I giggled. "It would be *absolutely* horrible." Then I reached over and swatted him on the head. "You know what I meant."

"I know what you meant." His smiled slowly vanished as he asked, "But what if we lasted more than six months? What if we lasted…years?"

I thought of how much pain I'd gone through with Adam when we were young. I had relived it so often over the years, the wounds had hardly had chance to heal. And here I was, potentially setting myself up for more.

Matching his more serious tone, I could say nothing other than what I'd always held true. "It would be worth losing everything…it would be more than worth it."

"It would be." His stare made me wobbly inside, and I was relieved when he looked down at his hands for a moment. He soon met my eyes again, though. "You know, Nicki, I don't have to stay in my job. I don't really even have to bloody work."

"I would never ask you to do that. Besides, your quitting really doesn't fix the appearances issue. I don't want to be a distraction in any way for Logan."

He rubbed his forehead, like I'd taken away his only good idea. "So what do you want to do?" he asked.

"Be your friend. See how that goes." Not that I really liked that idea.

"I can play that game, but…"

"But what?"

"Well, you said yourself we were never just friends."

"Yeah, but you were the one who said that we should try. Shouldn't we see if there's something lasting between us first — before we make a mess of things?"

"I get the logic, but I now see that it's harder than I thought."

"What do you mean?"

He laughed and shook his head. "For one thing, I feel like a seventeen-year-old boy again around you."

"Well, I certainly don't feel my age around you. I'm not an anxious person normally. I'm fairly self-confident. I don't wander around in a state of confusion, but now that you're here, it's like I'm a day-dreaming teenager with a hopeless crush on the most popular boy." I scowled at him. "And it's really fucking annoying — especially at work."

"It's harder for me."

"How so?"

"Seeing you…every day…looking so lovely. I just want to touch you all the time."

So he wanted to have sex with me? Well, I couldn't deny I wanted that with him, but it wasn't very romantic.

As if he read my mind, he slowly moved his hand over my cheek-bone and rubbed his thumb over my brow. It was so kind I rested my cheek in his hand. His eyes were fixed on mine as he declared, "I loved you, Nicki. And to my eyes, you're still the fairest of them all."

My eyes widened. What was there to say to that? "Adam…" I whispered.

"But now you're also this fascinating woman. I want to touch you, but I want more. I want to hear your stories. I want to listen to your opinions on things. I want to get to know you again."

"I loved you, too," I said, placing my hand on his for a moment. Simply acknowledging our past felt like such a relief. I smiled. "I also want to get to know you again."

"Actually, that's not my preference."

"Really?"

He slid his hand from my cheek, down my neck, and onto my shoulder. His expression became sly. "My preference would be to take you to my bed, shut the fucking door, and let no one see us for days. The rest of the world be damned."

"That sounds…fun," I said with a giggle, but I soon shook my head. "But the world is still out there, Adam. We can't do that."

Then Lisa called from inside, "Nicki? Adam? We're gonna watch a movie. Do you want to come inside?"

There was still so much more to say, but I needed a break. "I think we should go in. Is that okay?"

"That's fine. Though I hope she didn't let David choose the film. He has terrible taste."

"I'm so surprised to hear that." I grinned and called inside, "Yeah, Lisa. We're coming in."

When we walked into the living room, David was already changing channels. "I found something. *The Pineapple Express*. I like the sound of it."

"It sounds awful," Lisa said as she dimmed the lights.

"We don't have to pay attention, love," said David.

"Ha," she said.

Lisa and David sat on one sofa, with enough room between them that I could've joined them. Instead, I followed Adam to the other sofa. I kicked off my shoes and curled up safely into a corner, while Adam sat closer to the middle.

After only a few minutes, I heard Lisa mutter, "This is unwatchable. It's so bad."

Without saying anything else, she headed for the balcony, and David was right behind her. Out of the corner of my eye, I saw him touch her arm and nod toward the hallway leading to the bedrooms. Lisa answered sternly, "No way." She then said something I couldn't hear, and the two went out on the balcony.

I looked over and saw Adam watching them, too. I smiled, realizing we were alone on a sofa in a dark room. I wasn't ready for that in so many ways. But all my life I'd fallen asleep during movies, and at that moment, a nap seemed like the safest thing I could do. I closed my eyes and avoided everything—until I woke up an hour later.

As I got my bearings, I realized I was cozied right next to Adam. Damn subconscious.

He smiled at me. "Did you have a nice nap?"

"I can't believe I did that. I'm sorry." I sat up to move myself back to the corner.

"Don't worry about it. You were tired."

"No, really. I shouldn't have."

He pointed to the wet spot on the throw pillow.

"Oh God. I drooled."

"Don't worry about it."

"I'm so embarrassed. I—"

"Nicki, it's okay." He chuckled. "It's just me."

I cocked my head for a moment. It *was* him. It was Adam. After all these years and all those tears, Adam was beside me. Acting on instinct and certainly not reason, I leaned closer to him without thought of any consequences. I just knew what I wanted, and I wanted it now.

It started as a quick kiss, but I didn't want to let go. It had been too long. With my lips never leaving his, I straddled him and, sitting on his lap, cupped his cheeks with my hands. His mouth opened at once. Our tongues found each other, and what had started as a sweet kiss of remembrance turned into a ravishing. His hands were in my hair, his tongue teasing mine. Having spent a good part of my junior year of high school making out with Adam, kissing was something we did very well together. Only now, there was no youthful hesitancy or awkwardness. It was all fire and want—though controlled. Knowing that Lisa was somewhere nearby, I knew things couldn't get out of hand.

Yet they did when Adam grabbed my ass, pulling me toward him. As he gave me tender kisses all along my neck, he positioned me astride his bulging erection, and I gladly pressed against him. Even with the damn clothes between us, I loved feeling him, but when he started to thrust, I froze in shock. What was I doing? Of course, my body wanted to have sex right then and there, but that wasn't the right thing to do for anyone.

I placed my forehead on his and found my breath. "I...I'm sorry, Adam. I shouldn't have let this happen. It's not right."

"Not right? Are you sure?"

"No...I'm not sure about anything." I pulled away and looked at him dead on. His brown eyes drooped a little. I couldn't have that. Even though he'd put me smack-dab in the middle of a personal and professional quagmire, I was too happy for him to ever be sad. He had to know. "Wait. That's not true. I'm sure about one thing."

"And what's that?" He was such a sourpuss.

"That I want to spend more time with you." I ran my hand through his thick hair. "*That* I know for sure."

"Well, get some control, woman," he grumbled with a smile. "Get off me before you kiss me again."

I giggled and tousled his hair again. He'd switched channels to a replay of a UK soccer game—Chelsea versus Tottenham. Off-handedly, I mentioned a guy I had dated in college who was a Chelsea fan.

"I hate him," Adam said with a sneer.

"Why?"

"Because he dated you when I couldn't and he's a fan of the most God-awful annoying team in the Premier League."

"Juan Carlos likes soccer, too. I can't remember who he likes in the UK. I get the names confused. Maybe Arsenal?"

"Even worse! Why did you tell me that? Now I really hate the short-arse!"

"Short?" Is that really what Adam thought of him? Someone had once made a short joke about Juan Carlos to me, and it was all I could do not to tell him that Juan Carlos was anything but short where it really counted. That wasn't the right thing to say to Adam, though. "Come on. Not every guy towers over the world like you."

"Why are we talking about him?"

"I don't know."

"Let's change the subject."

"Yes, let's." I poked his arm. "You know, I still have that Liverpool scarf you gave me."

"You do? I'd forgotten about that."

The way he'd said it made me think he was lying. There was no way he'd forgotten giving me that. The man was obsessed with Liverpool.

David and Lisa then walked back in the room, and David soon spotted the TV. "Football? Why didn't you tell me?"

"I should've," said Adam. "Nicki's a Liverpool fan."

I jabbed him in the ribs while David praised me. Lisa kept rubbing her neck like she needed a break, so I suggested we call it a night.

Everyone agreed. When David walked her over to the foyer, I could tell he wanted to talk to her again.

Adam winked at me, and I pointed to the hallway where our friends were and whispered, "I want to listen."

He nodded, and we could hear Lisa say, "We have absolutely nothing in common."

"After that kiss, I'm pretty sure we'll have the most important thing in common," said David.

I looked up at Adam and dropped my mouth open in surprise. He gave a nod like he was impressed with his cousin.

"Whatever," Lisa said. "You can't base a relationship on that."

"Are you kidding, princess?" said David. "It's the key to any successful relationship."

"Well, he's right," Adam said into my ear.

"I suppose so." I giggled, turning my attention away from them.

Adam touched my hair and said, "I should leave before you attack me again."

"I think I can control myself." What a silly girl I was. Our eyes met for a second, and my hormones kicked in. I leaned over and kissed his cheek. "Now get outta here."

Chapter Nine

The following night, I still had the phone to my ear when my line went dead. Juan Carlos had all but hung up on me. Tossing the phone to my side, I rose from the sofa and then headed to Lisa's room. She sat in the middle of her bed with an array of scientific journals around her.

"How was it?" she asked, removing her glasses.

"Awful," I said as I moved a journal aside so I could sit. The title was the Centers for Disease Control and Prevention's *Morbidity and Mortality Weekly Report*. It was fitting for my mood.

"What did he say?"

"That I was too career driven."

"Huh?" She wrinkled her brow. "I thought you told him about Adam."

"Sort of."

"Oh God. Why didn't you tell him everything?"

"I'm not ready to. It doesn't feel right. I still love him, and I have no idea what's going to happen with Adam." I opened up the mortality report as if it had my life's answers. "He brought up Adam, though."

"Start at the beginning, please." She took a sip of the tea on her nightstand and leaned on her pillow. "This doesn't make sense."

"It will." I sighed. "When I told him I didn't think it was right to move in together because we spent so little time in the same city, he got a little annoyed like I was blaming him because he travels so much. I told him I loved him, that I've been traveling just as much, and he knows even when we're in town, I still have a shitty schedule."

"True, but when you two decided to move in together, you knew that would be the situation."

"That's what he said. He said something has changed with me. He asked if it had anything to do with my spending time with Adam."

"And what did you say?"

"I said I'm having a great time in DC and working my ass off. I'm not sure that I want to settle down right now."

"Nicki…"

"Well, it's true. Nothing may come of Adam and me."

"True, but you did make out with him last night."

"You're crazy if you think I'm telling Juan Carlos that," I said, shaking my head furiously.

"So you lied to him."

"Not really." I cringed. "And I'm going to try not to."

"But as of today, you are officially stringing him along. You can't be *in* love with one person while making out with another."

"I don't think it's so black and white," I said, trying to reason my way out of what was a very good point. "As I said—"

She let out a low laugh and put her hand on my arm. "It's okay. I'm not the press. You don't need to spin me. Remember, I'm on your side, whatever you do. You could commit murder and I'd be right there with you."

"But you think I'm a bad person, right?"

"Nah," she said, reaching over to her nightstand for her wine. She took a sip and declared, "You're just confused."

"Yup. I am."

Throughout the next few weeks at work, I tried to be cooler with Adam, but it was like he could tell I was overcompensating. He had this permanent smirk whenever our eyes met. I'd have to turn away so I didn't smile.

On a Friday, he cornered me with his reporter's notepad, a very handy prop for our ruse. "Good morning, Nicki."

"Good morning," I said, clutching my own prop, my cell phone.

"So your big date is tomorrow?"

"You mean the Correspondents' Dinner?"

"Yes. Are you still going with Juan Carlos?"

"Of course. I told you I was."

"What makes him so special that he has to have two names?"

I snorted. Two could play at this little game. "What about Felicity? What kind of name is that anyway? It's not a name. Happiness is a state of being. Are *you* still taking her to the dinner?"

"Yes." The smirk vanished, and he waved his notebook like he was fending me off. "I'll see you tomorrow."

I glared at his back as he walked away, but his fast pace tipped me off that I shouldn't be annoyed with him. The guy was jealous, and I knew exactly how he felt.

When Juan Carlos picked me up for the White House Correspondents' Dinner, he couldn't have been the more perfect date. He looked scorching hot in his tux, and he presented me with a lovely little bouquet. Finally, he dipped me for a kiss, which made me giggle, but before he went in for it he said, "You're right. We should enjoy ourselves more."

I touched my finger to his nose. "When we're together, and when we're apart."

I'd meant for it to be lighthearted, but he frowned and said, "If you say so." There was no sweeping kiss after that, just a peck and a grouchy date.

Walking into the giant hotel ballroom, I looked around for Adam. As much as I didn't want to see him with Felicity, I was curious about her. At such a big event, though, it was impossible for me to find them.

I suppose I could've hunted down the BBC table, but while the event was all fun and games for everyone else in the room, I was working. Luckily, President Logan was a hit that evening as he roasted his friends and foes, and they did the same to him. I was pleased because we'd rehearsed his jokes, and they all came off naturally.

After the dinner, I had to work the room, but Juan Carlos didn't seem to mind. I left him with one of his big clients and made my rounds with the reporters and celebrities. It took me a bit before I saw Adam staring at me. I patted the arm of a congresswoman I'd been talking to and headed straight toward him.

"Good evening," he said. He gave me a blatant up-and-down appraisal. Nearly sixteen years later, I still didn't have any cleavage, but at least I'd found some curves along the way. I was also still thin enough to wear something slinky. The dress had a halter-top that forgivingly hid my flat chest, but the silver silk charmeuse clung to the rest of me. "You look ravishing."

"Thanks." Somehow his compliment meant more than when Juan Carlos had said it, and I got shy. "You look dashing…as ever."

"Thanks." He grinned. "Think you can control yourself this time?"

"You're such a fucking arse," I said, swatting his arm.

Holding up his hands, he pretended to protect himself. "I always loved it when you cursed."

Then a woman's voice with a posh British accent came from behind. "What's this? Attacking the press?"

Felicity. Filled with fear and curiosity, I turned to finally see her. In stilettos, she was as tall as Adam and wore a strapless blue dress that her breasts spilled out of. She had one of those long, narrow English faces and perfect skin. I tried to find a flaw, but I couldn't.

As she placed her hand on Adam's shoulder, he stiffened, but his perfect aristocratic manners took over. "Hello, Felicity. This is Nicole Johnson." He turned to me. "Nicole, this is Felicity Chambers."

Felicity side-eyed him, and he scratched his temple for a second. "Lady Felicity Chambers, I should say."

"I normally don't use the title," she said with a smile.

Though you don't mind throwing it around, I thought. I extended my hand. "It's nice to meet you. I've seen some of your work on TV."

"Yes," she said, barely shaking my hand. I hated wimpy hand-shakes. I saw it as a sign of insincerity or timidity, neither of which I liked. "As I've seen you," she said and then smiled at Adam. "Of course, Adam has mentioned you before."

"We've known each other for a while," I said, gripping my clutch. *Dear God, get me out of here.*

"So he's said." She removed her hand from his shoulder and clasped her hands. "He told me of your upbringing. I think it's such an endearing story about how you came from nothing, and now look at you. You're at the height of government. Truly amazing."

Huh? Rarely did my facial expressions betray my feelings—I was a cool cucumber—but at that moment, I leaned back and my face spoke for me. *What the fuck?* My parents were both lawyers; I had an upper-middle class upbringing in embarrassingly bourgeois Bellaire, Texas. Did she speak for Adam? It was what I'd always expected his father thought of me, but Adam had never been that way. I flashed him a look and saw he had the same expression as me.

"Fel, I never said that. Nicki's family is highly educated and somewhat well-to-do."

"Oh, you know what I mean," she said with a wave of her hand.

"I suppose our notions of class are different in the US." I should've left it at that, but my sharp tongue lashed out. "We're a meritocracy and don't look down on the middle class."

"Oh, I'm not looking down on you. I think it's a rather heartwarming story."

"I actually think it's pretty boring." I laughed with no mirth at all. "But maybe it's similar to how Americans admire British royalty though we would never want any ourselves."

"Wouldn't you now? I think Americans are obsessed with the monarchy."

"Obsessed? Only in a celebrity-gossip way." I arched a brow and couldn't let it go. "You have to admit picking the firstborn kid of the firstborn kid of the firstborn kid of an inbred family is a lousy way to choose a head of state."

"Now, Nicole," she said with a simpering look. "You're smart enough to know we have a constitutional monarchy."

My head snapped to Adam, whose eyes were wide in horror whereas I was ticked. "Actually," I said turning my attention back to her. "I'm even smart enough to know that despite your constitutional monarchy, the Queen is still the head of state."

"I suppose you are trained in protocol in your position."

Adam clapped his hands. "Felicity, pardon me. I need to speak to Nicole alone for a moment about a story I'm working on."

"But of course." She gave me one more haughty smile. "It was a pleasure to meet you."

"And you," I said.

Adam waited until she'd walked a few feet away and began talking with a Greek shipping magnate, Gus Papadopoulos, before he led me to a corner.

I looked over his shoulder to see her throwing her head back in laughter. I doubted the old Greek dude was that funny. "That was interesting," I muttered.

"I'm so sorry," he said.

"Did you think you had a cat fight on your hands?"

"More like the start of an international incident." He wiped his brow. "She must feel incredibly threatened by you to speak that way."

"And she's otherwise charming?"

"Maybe not charming." He laughed. "But she's a smart reporter. She knows you don't piss off someone who has the ear of the president of the United States."

"You have horrible taste in women, you know. Always have."

"Only when I'm biding my time waiting for you to come around."

I craned my neck again to see Felicity continuing her flirty chat with the Greek. I was nothing like that woman. "Clearly, I was an anomaly."

"In the best way."

I met Adam's eyes again and remarked, "Her breasts are certainly on display for you and everyone else in the room."

"Are you jealous, Nicki Johnson?"

"No!" I scrunched my face. "Maybe."

"Good. Now you know how I feel about fucking Juan Carlos."

"Remember I spent a good part of my junior year of high school jealous as hell because you were with Meredith Daniels."

"Was that her name? I'd forgotten."

My eyes wandered around the room. "If we weren't under the surveillance of stupid Dan Roark right now, I'd punch you in the arm for that."

"Sorry. I'd deserve it if you did." He leaned in closer to me. "You know, you're the one I've remembered."

I exhaled and smiled but didn't reply. I just wanted to soak in the moment.

After a while, he cleared his throat. "Are you going home with him?"

"Juan Carlos?"

"*Si, Juan Carlos*," he said in an exaggerated Spanish accent. "Who else?"

"There's no one else. You know that."

"So then, Juan Carlos, or JC. Are you taking him home?"

I touched my neck in emotional panic. "He usually stays with me, but I don't know. He's not too happy with me right now. We could very well end up in another fight." I returned his deadpan stare. "Are you going home with her?"

"She usually stays with me." He shook his head. "After her little run-in with you, I'd say we're guaranteed to have a fight."

"Good." My hand flew to my mouth. I couldn't believe I'd said it aloud, but I still smiled.

Before I could cover up my faux pas, he grinned. "I feel the same way."

As soon as I walked away from him, I found Juan Carlos, who gave me the silent treatment. It was my own damn fault. I'd talked to Adam for too long.

For the rest of the night, Juan Carlos was animated when talking with everyone else but a complete turd when he spoke with me. It was only when we were in the cab headed to my place that he let loose. "What did you and Adam talk about?"

"I don't know…" There wasn't a sentence I could relay that wouldn't tip him off. Then I thought of my unlikely savior. "His girlfriend was there."

"Uh huh." He didn't buy it.

It was an untenable situation. I couldn't and shouldn't tell him my every thought and word with Adam, but I hated lying. I took a sharp breath and said, "I love you, Juan Carlos, but can't I be friends with Adam?"

"I love you, but I promise you he wants to be more than friends." He gave me a side-glance and looked out the window. "And don't pretend like you don't know it."

Everyone always said women had intuition, but men had the uncanny ability to sense when another man was horning in on his mate. I deflected again. "Felicity would have something to say about that."

He clasped my hand in his. "I love you, I'll fight for you, but I'm not going to be part of any kind of scandal."

"Thanks, but neither am I." *Because I will never let it get to that point...*

"I think we should take a break for a bit."

I blinked repeatedly, not believing what I was hearing. Juan Carlos was breaking up with me in a cab? I looked at the driver, who was talking at warp speed in Farsi on his phone. At least we had some privacy.

I was confused. "You just said you love me and want to fight for me."

"I do, but I think you need some space."

"So this is actually a break, not a break-up?"

"Yes."

"All right." My forehead furrowed. "If that's what you want." Now that it was being handed to me, I wasn't sure if I wanted this new-found freedom.

He nodded, and with a quick flick of his wrist, he checked his watch. "I can't spend the night tonight. My stuff is at Jeff's, and I've got an early flight."

"Okay," I said, though I knew in my bones everything was far from okay with him. Yet despite the uneasiness, a wave of relief came over me. I wasn't going to have to choose that night.

Chapter Ten

The next day, there was no better means for me to get my mind off my personal life than to head in to work. As I typed away in my quiet office, I heard my phone buzz with a text. It was Adam.

Morning, Nicki. How are you?

I smiled and replied.

Good morning. I'm at work. What are you up to?

His response made me jealous.

Reading the paper. Then working. Then playing football.

The life of a reporter was easier than mine, I grumbled to myself.

That sounds fun.

Then he proved Juan Carlos right.

Can I see you this week?

I typed with a smile on my face.

Check your calendar! We're traveling starting Wednesday. We'll see each other all the time.

It took him a moment to write back.

Smart-arse. You know what I meant.

I giggled aloud.

I know :) Let's see how it goes. It's a busy week.

I stared at my phone. Texting with Adam was much more fun than work.

BTW, you looked beautiful last night.

My hand went to my cheeks.

You're making me blush.

Then he told me something he'd once said before, a long time ago.

Good. You're even prettier when you blush.
Now crack on with your work.

Of course, any trip to the Midwest electoral battleground states for an American president was of the most critical importance. With the region's aging industries of steel production, coal mining, and car manufacturing, the economy was fragile. I never got a moment to spare until the second night. I decided to call Adam on the hotel phone just to surprise him.

"Hello," he said.

"Hi, Adam. It's Nicki."

"Well, hello. Why are you calling me on the hotel phone?"

"For kicks. Did I surprise you?"

"A little bit. Actually, it reminds me that we're in the same building."

"We are," I said, looking around my room.

"Which floor are you on?"

"The twenty-second. And you?"

"I'm on the twentieth. We're neighbors."

"Not really. My neighbors are Secret Service snipers on either side of me."

"Snipers? I never really thought about the president traveling with snipers."

"Well, he does—in case they need to easily kill someone trying to kill him. You're not supposed to see them, though."

"That is the job of a sniper." He laughed. "So should I be looking at the rooftops and belfries to find them?"

"Yeah, during the day when the president is outside, that's a good place to start. Right now, you could just wander along the twenty-second floor. Both of those guys have the TV blaring in their rooms. They'd be easy to locate."

"And so I could figure out that your room is the quiet one in between theirs?"

"Yeah…"

"I'm coming up, then."

"What?" I panicked.

"Scared you, didn't I?" He laughed.

"Maybe."

"You have to admit it's a bit frustrating we're finally talking and even in the same building, but we're not in the same room."

"Yeah, but…" I giggled. "I don't think being in a hotel room alone together is a good idea."

"Now, why would that be? We would just talk…well, I would just talk. Considering your behavior the other night, I'd have to fend you off."

"You're never going to let me live that down, are you?"

"No, I won't." He lowered his voice. "So you never told me what happened with old Juan Carlos."

I thought about Juan Carlos's warning of a scandal. I didn't want to bring it up, so I kept it short and turned the tables. "We're taking a little break. What about Felicity?" I chuckled. "I mean Lady Felicity."

"Now, be nice…"

"You've got to be kidding me after the crap she said to me."

"You don't need to be angry with her. I'm angry enough for both of us, and I gave her a right bollocking."

"So did you kiss and make up?" I hit my hand on my forehead. I didn't want an answer.

"Not really." He cleared his throat. "Do you actually want to talk about this?"

"Not really," I muttered.

"Seriously, Nicki, I want to see you again. When can we spend some time together? Next weekend?"

"Um, I'd like that, but my dad visits next weekend."

"That's nice."

"Yeah, he's coming for a visit. He arrives on Friday morning and leaves Sunday afternoon."

"Will you two be going out with Juan Carlos?"

"No." I sighed. "Given what's going on with Juan Carlos and me right now, I don't think it's appropriate to go out with my dad together. There'd just be too much expectation around it."

"Ah. Okay."

Somehow his mild manner encouraged me to explain more. "It's weird, you know. I never understood until now how people could be separated. I never got how that worked. I always thought you were either in a relationship or out of one—on or off. Now that I'm in the middle, I understand a little more. It's not a comfortable place. No one wants to be there. Things aren't working. But you don't want to do anything drastic yet, so you feel like you're just buying time until you can make a decision."

"Er. Yeah."

"Oh God, Adam. I'm sorry. I'm rambling."

"No. No need to apologize. Actually, I was in a similar situation with Muff."

"Muff? Really?"

"My ex-girlfriend. We were together for a few years. The difference here is that you've been honest with Juan Carlos. You asked for time apart while still being together. I didn't ask with Muff. I just took the time without telling her why."

"It was actually more of a mutual decision between Juan Carlos and me, and we sort of glossed over why, although your name came up."

"In a bad way?"

I really didn't want to dwell on Juan Carlos. "Tell me more about this Muff person."

"Not much to say. She really wanted to get married. I didn't. It was an ugly break-up."

"And your parents wanted you to get married?"

"Dad was eager for me to marry her. But my mum, being a counselor, always said she wanted what I wanted. She's good that way."

"That must've been difficult with your dad."

"It was."

I did feel sorry for Adam's strained relationship with his father. I didn't want to make him sad about it, though, so I asked, "You really dated a woman named Muff?"

"It's a family nickname. Her real name is Mary."

"In America, 'muff' is slang."

"Now, Nicki, what's it slang for?"

"You figure it out." I giggled.

"I'd like to."

"And what do you mean by that?"

"I suppose it's not fair for me to say things like that to you." He was smug. "I don't want to be a tease."

"Oh God. Can we move on?"

"Of course. So how was today?"

"It sucked. The schedule was a disaster. The meetings went poorly. Logan was cranky. And I spent most of my day responding to an idiot congressman who likened Logan to friggin' Fidel Castro for bailing out the US automakers."

"Well, when I think of Communists, I definitely think of rabid free-traders like Logan."

"I know. It's ridiculous. A giant portion of the American economy is linked to car manufacturing. Any president would bail them out in some way."

"Other than your boss being compared to a crazy Communist dictator, did anything good happen today?"

"I got to talk to you," I said with a smile.

"That is a good thing. So next weekend…when does your father leave?"

"I could see you Sunday afternoon."

"Good. Come and see me after my football match. David will be there. After the game, we all go out as a group. They're nice blokes, and it's such a large group you shouldn't worry about us being seen out together."

It sounded like fun and not a heavy date in public. "Should I bring Lisa?" She'd been extraordinarily tight-lipped about David, only saying he was a good kisser and an even better bullshit artist.

"I'm sure David would like that. He says he's chipping away at her. I'm willing to bet he's already asked her out."

"I bet she's said no, too. I'll bring her along, though."

"Meet us at the pitch. We play at the polo fields on the Mall near the tidal basin. Do you know where that is?"

"Yeah. I've been there once before when Juan Carlos played a game."

"JC plays football?"

"Occasionally."

"Tosser. He's probably lousy."

"No, he isn't for your information." His jealousy was amusing. "And what do you mean by 'tosser'? He doesn't use his hands when he plays."

Adam snickered, which let me know I'd said something ridiculous. "Never mind," he said. "You should get some sleep. I'd offer to tuck you in, but…"

"Good night, Adam."

"Night, Nicki."

For the next few days, Adam and I exchanged a few texts and talked a few times, but that was it. My dad came in to town for work in the middle of the week, and I arranged my schedule so we could spend time together. On Friday morning, we'd planned for him to attend a press briefing. He was also going to get to say hello to Logan, which he was really excited about.

After the briefing, I spoke with my dad off to the side, and a few reporters came up to me and asked if he was my father. I was really hoping Adam had left the room, but he hadn't. When the crowd cleared, he started toward me. I hadn't told my dad about him yet. When I'd finally mentioned it to my mom, it had turned into a complete replay of my very first conversation with Lisa when she'd grilled me. Not fun. So I'd avoided talking at any length with my mom since then, and this was definitely not the time to spring Adam on my dad. I gave Adam a slight shake of my head and hurried my dad off to see the president.

Unfortunately, that wasn't the end. Dad's meeting with Logan was all of five minutes—they might've been old friends, but Logan was the leader of the free world and it was a workday. So afterward, I took him on a tour around the White House grounds.

As we strolled along, Adam appeared out of nowhere. "Good morning, Nicki."

"Oh…uh. Morning, Adam." I sucked in some air and gave him a determined smile. "Adam, this is my father, Kevin Johnson. Dad, this is Adam Kincaid…with the BBC."

"It's a pleasure to meet you, sir," Adam said as he extended his hand.

Dad's brow furrowed for a moment, but soon his prosecutor poker face took over and he began his interrogation. "Good morning, Adam. Your name. It sounds familiar. Why is that?"

Because my dad had already moved to Chicago by my junior year, he'd never met Adam, but he certainly knew about him. If this were my mother meeting Adam again, she'd be gushing over him. But since Dad only knew the bad parts about our relationship, this was tougher.

I went for a vague explanation. "Dad, Adam lived in Bellaire for a while when I was in high school."

Dad broke eye contact with him and glanced at me. He was obviously putting two and two together, but Adam was the one to break the silence and acknowledge everything. "Meeting Nicki was the best part of my year in the States."

I faked a glance at my watch. "Yeah, that was a fun year. Dad, we need to get going if you're going to get to your lunch in Alexandria."

He nodded quietly. "Nice to meet you, Adam." Then his eyes darted over to me, and he added, "After all these years."

"Yes, you too, sir. Enjoy your holiday." He turned to me. "Bye, Nicki."

"So long." I avoided his eyes and gladly steered my dad toward the gate.

On Sunday, Lisa and I showed up at the soccer field toward the end of the game. The guys were on the field, and memories of watching Adam play soccer in high school flooded back to me. I'd loved watching him play, but seeing him in his uniform was even better. Both teams were like a study in international diplomacy, and English was just one of the languages spoken on the field. The others included Spanish, German, French, Arabic, and a few I didn't know at all.

Lisa and I weren't obvious in the crowded sidelines, and I wondered if Adam knew I was there to see him dribble the ball down the field, pass it to David, and watch David make a goal. Just as the ball went into the goal, David dropped down to his knee and ripped off his shirt before running around like a madman hugging everyone in sight.

"That's the only time he's going to score with me around."

"You can stop now. Admit it. He's adorable."

"He has his moments," she said, letting a smile escape.

"Have you seen him with his shirt off before?"

"No."

"So what do you think?"

"I think he's damn fine." She gave me a warning glare. "Don't tell him I said that."

"No way. I'm not messing up this game of cat and mouse."

After the game ended, Adam and David headed for the sidelines, with Adam stripping off his jersey as he walked. Adam half-naked was a sight to see and not one I was ready for.

I turned away, and Lisa laughed at me. "I guess you haven't seen Adam with his shirt off either."

"Not recently."

"And what do you think?"

I smiled and bit my knuckle. "Let's just say he's filled out."

David's voice carried across the field. "Did you see my goal, princess?"

"I did," Lisa said matter-of-factly. When they walked up, she smirked and teasingly ran a finger down David's chest and showed the sweat on her finger to him. "You need a shower."

He grabbed her like he was going to dance with her. "Only if you'll join me."

"Gross! Don't touch me." She pushed him back. "You stink."

"You're a doctor. You're not supposed to mind the human body."

"I don't, but I prefer them clean."

As David and Lisa bantered away, Adam said to me, "Thanks for coming out here."

"Thanks for the invitation." I smiled but didn't look at him. How could I? At the moment, he was the stuff of my fantasies.

We chatted for a bit, and all the while, I kept my eyes everywhere but on him.

Eventually, he said, "I hate to be presumptuous like my incorrigible cousin, but I do get the feeling you're averting your eyes."

"No. Why would you say that?" I covered my mouth to hide my smile.

"So it's not because I'm standing here half-naked?"

"Can you not say that word?" I asked, laughing.

"Oh, forgive me. I know how difficult this must be for you."

I rolled my eyes. "Will you please just put on a shirt?"

"Sure. Give me a second." He grabbed a towel from his bag and began to dry himself off. *Oh my God.* I stared at the very top of his head, and he noticed. He nodded across the field and said, "You can look over there if this gets to be too much."

"Whatever."

I peeked to see what he was wearing and saw a Liverpool sweatshirt. Perfect. In shorts, sneakers, and a University of Chicago sweatshirt, I'd dressed no worse than him.

After he was fully clothed again, he grinned and tousled my ponytail. "When your hair is tied up like this, you look seventeen again."

"I don't think so," I said, though I was pleased. I got sick of dressing up for work during the week, so I put my hair up a lot on the weekends.

"You're prettier now, though."

The man always had the ability to be so charming he left me speechless. I tentatively touched my ponytail and felt the need to return the compliment, though after that cocky display of his, I didn't want to go too far. "Well, you don't look seventeen anymore either."

"Are you saying I look old?"

"No." I laughed. "You've just…changed since then."

"Ah! Not how you remember me? Not a skinny lad anymore?" He leaned against a post lining the field. "And you like that, do you now?"

I pretended to look at the sky. "Doo-dee-doo. I'm not answering that."

"I'm sorry. It was cruel of me to bring it up given your inability to keep your hands to yourself."

"That joke only has so much life in it."

"Not if you pounce on me again."

"Believe me, I can control myself."

"It's good that one of us can," he said with a wink.

We drove our separate cars up to a dive Mexican joint on the outskirts of Adams Morgan. Both teams came along, and it was a giant, loud table that only grew bigger as many of the players' girlfriends and friends arrived. No one could tell where Adam and I fit in the picture, and it helped that many of them didn't speak English.

As drinks arrived, David began to teach the Swedes and Germans how to do tequila shots. I already had a margarita and needed to keep some of my wits about me, but Lisa was at David's side, debating whether or not to do one. He raised another glass and said sexily, "Have you ever done a body shot, love?"

She sneered. "You know, I'm not one of your little playthings."

"Don't be offended, love. It was a joke." He chuckled. "The first time I lick you certainly won't be in public."

"Like there's going to be a first time." She crossed her arms emphatically.

As though realizing he'd screwed up, David moved his seat a little closer to her and leaned in to whisper in her ear. What he said, I didn't know, but by her annoyed expression, she wasn't impressed.

"David needs to go back to spending time with Lisa alone," I said to Adam. "He might've done some permanent damage trying to show her off."

"I'm sure she'll forgive him." The twinkle appeared again in his eyes. "Maybe we could do a body shot?"

"Ha!"

"Well, say we were at a beach in Mexico and you were in a bikini…"

I couldn't even imagine it. Taking a sip of margarita, I muttered, "I don't wear bikinis, for starters."

"Why ever not?" He gave my frame an approving once-over. "You've got a great body."

What should've been a compliment was a crushing blow to me. He'd forgotten. I couldn't believe it. After the car accident in high school, my body had always been a huge issue for me. It was entirely covered in horrible scars, especially my torso. The few on my arms had become less obvious over time, though, and I was usually in long sleeves anyway. The gashes across my middle had likewise lost their deep purple hue, but they were still noteworthy both in number and color. Today, everything was fine as long as I kept my clothes on. I folded my arms over my stomach and mumbled, "My scars."

His smile fell. "Nicki, I'm so sorry. I'm such a bloody idiot. I swear I haven't forgotten. It just came out because you're so pretty and—"

"Don't worry about it. I wouldn't expect you to remember." It was the nice thing to say even if it wasn't true. "It's not a big deal."

"How could I forget? I didn't, I promise. I—"

"Please, let's just drop it. It really doesn't matter."

I took another sip of my drink and looked around the table, hoping there was a different conversation to join in. But then I felt his arm around my shoulder, pulling me to his side. He kissed the top of my head and murmured in my hair. "I told you many times I didn't care about a few silly scars. I still don't."

I winced, thinking of all those times he'd been so kind to me about my body when I'd been so horrified by it. I leaned into him for just a moment, enjoying his support once again. I remembered we were in public, though, and quickly straightened in my seat. I gave him a quick smile. "Thanks."

"I mean it."

I believed him, encouraging me once again to say something more. "It's not the scars themselves that are the problem. I mean, I've still got some visible ones." I pulled up my sleeve and pointed to the silvery lines on my arm. "They've faded, but they're still noticeable if you look hard, but I don't care anymore what I look like anyway. It's having to explain what happened that's the pain in the ass. People don't ask much about my arms. It's only when they see my stomach, where it's obvious something bad happened. They ask a lot of questions about those."

"And who *would* want to answer those questions?"

"Not me. That's the funny thing about leaving Bellaire and growing up. Outside of home, no one knows my history. There's no terrible tragedy. But when they see my scars, I have to explain it all. Unfortunately, they're still bad enough that people ask if everyone in the accident came out okay."

"That's hard," he said with a grimace.

"Yeah, a little. The thing that really bugs me, though, is when people hear about the accident and one of the first things they say is, 'I thought you were an only child.' It sounds so weird to me. I've spent half my life now without my sister, but I still can't think of myself as an only child." I sighed with a smile. "Anyway, that's why I don't wear a bikini. It's not really that I care how I look."

"Well, you look great," he said, squeezing my hand. "And you're not an only child. You're forever a bossy older sister. Except now you just boss around the entire White House Press Corps, including one BBC reporter."

"Yeah, right." I laughed.

He took a sip of his beer. "You don't have to tell me if you don't want to, but what was that with your father on Friday? It seemed like an odd conversation."

"It was."

"What happened?"

Ugh. Thinking back to my dad's reaction, I dreaded bringing up bad history. "I don't want to talk about it right now."

"Why not?"

"It's about after you left and…" I ran out of words.

"Nicki, I don't want to talk about when I left either, but if we're going to move forward, I think we need to…at least once."

"Okay, but not tonight. Not here."

"When?"

"Next weekend. Come over on Saturday." I cracked a smile and nodded toward David. "And bring him. He'll probably still be in the doghouse."

"You've got a date, then."

"It's not a date," I said, waving my finger at him.

"Okay. It's not a date. It's dinner at an old friend's."

"Exactly."

The following weekend, I was in the kitchen again while Lisa welcomed Adam and David into the apartment. David was flirty as usual with Lisa, and she put him off. Then I heard Adam say, "Where's Nicki?"

"In the kitchen, cooking," said Lisa.

"She didn't have to cook. She worked all day. I told her just to order takeaway."

"I said the same thing, but she wanted to cook."

When they entered the kitchen, I looked up from my pot of pasta sauce. Adam grinned at the apron I wore with my dress. He walked right over and kissed me on the cheek. "Evening."

"Hi." I smiled. "It's good to see you."

He peered into the steamy pot. "Hmm. Tomato sauce for pasta?"

"Hence the apron. It's a little messy."

"You look lovely tonight," he said, touching my arm.

"Thanks." The man just brought the shyness out of me sometimes. I handed him the spoon. "You stir. I need to get the pasta going."

The four of us spent the evening eating, drinking, and laughing. Over the course of dinner, David appeared to wear Lisa down. He'd brought her champagne because of her recent article in *The New England Journal of Medicine*.

After we cleared the dessert dishes, she shooed Adam and me out of the kitchen again. I protested because the place was a mess, but Lisa refused to listen. "It's okay. You cooked. I'll clean."

"And I'll help," said David.

"Good," she said. "It will keep your hands busy."

"I need that around you, angel."

"Let's go outside," Adam said, sounding a little tired of David's shtick.

"Sure." We both had our wine glasses at hand, but I knew I'd need more to make it through the conversation. I grabbed a full bottle of wine.

"The whole bottle?" he asked with a smile.

"If we have to talk, I might need it."

Putting his arm around my shoulder, he laughed. "I might need it, too." When we got out on the balcony, I headed straight to the railing, but he tugged at my arm. Gesturing to the chaise lounge, he said, "Over here this time."

I halted for a moment. Adam wasn't wasting any time. That same feeling I'd had in high school came over me. He was moving a little faster than I was ready for, but I couldn't say no to him. "Oh…okay."

He lay down, taking me with him. It was so comfortable that I curled up next to him, and he kept an arm around me. "Now this is more like it," he said.

"It's nice."

"It's more than nice."

"You're right." I sighed. "I'm sorry we didn't talk much this week."

"We were both busy." He became hesitant. "What's going on with Juan Carlos?"

"We're in touch, though not like before." My answer begged a question of him. "And Felicity?"

"She's been sent on assignment to Indonesia. We haven't been talking much because of that."

"Only because of that?" I started to worry.

"No, of course not." He squeezed my arm. "I think the fact we're together is a sign there are other reasons."

I grinned and nuzzled into his side, and out of the silence, he asked, "So what about your dad? What does he know of me?"

"It seems so long ago." I hated dredging up what I'd kept down for so long, so I told him the bare minimum. "Well, after you were gone, I hated being in Bellaire. I didn't spend much time with my friends when I was there, and I ended up at Dad's in Chicago a lot."

"So that's how he knows me? You talked?"

"No, not really. He must've gotten your name from Mom. That's why your name rang a bell with him. He never forgets anything."

"He must not. He wasn't overly friendly."

"Oh, don't worry about him. He was surprised to see you, but I was the one he interrogated."

"What did you say about us…now?"

"That we're friends." I was coy. "Close friends."

"And did he believe you?"

"At first…but when I told him Juan Carlos and I were taking a break, he became suspicious. He warned me up, down, and sideways about what might happen to me professionally and also to Logan."

"So he probably doesn't think much of me."

"Dad doesn't think much of anyone. He's innately suspicious."

"So why did you spend so much time with him in high school?"

"Because he left me alone."

Adam nodded and was silent for a moment. I could hear him swallow hard before he said, "Yeah, for a while all I wanted to do was be alone — from the moment I left your house. I remember I went home, where my family was waiting for me beside the hired car we took to the airport. I must've looked like utter shit from crying." He tapped my rear. "And from rolling around in bed with you all night."

"Yeah, we did some of that, didn't we?" I giggled.

"My God. We did a lot of that. Every damn day."

"I know, all the time. Now that I'm older and look back…well…" I smirked. "We had a lot of hormones then."

He laughed. "I'd say I'm struggling with my hormones right now."

"Yeah, I know the feeling," I muttered.

"Maybe I should get back to my story."

"Good idea."

"So…when my family saw me, they didn't say anything about me being out all night or even my appearance. They let me sleep, so I slept in the car and for most of the flight back to England. When I got home, I was still sad. I missed you terribly."

He straightened a bit, and his expression became intense. "Just so you know, I never got back together with Kate — at all — ever. In fact, I didn't have a relationship with anyone for a long time."

Wow. I'd always wondered if he'd gone back to Kate. The answer was music to my ears, but I only nodded, and he continued on. "Even when I did start seeing people again, I tried to keep up with you from the bits of information I got from Sylvia."

"And then?"

"Then when Logan was running for president, I occasionally saw you in the press. And when he was elected and appointed you a press secretary, I asked for the White House job. You know the rest."

It was time for my confession. I needed to own up to my part in the break-up. "I'm sorry I put both of us through that. I just couldn't handle any more pain. I was confident that if I saw you, we'd just break up again. I knew I couldn't take it. I'm sorry. It was mean of me…I was selfish…I was all those things you called me before you left for your grandfather's funeral."

"I won't have you apologizing to me, Nicki. I was an immature boy and cruel to you."

"But I've wanted to apologize. I don't think things would've changed between us, but it was awful of me to ignore you. I've felt so guilty."

"Please don't. Looking back, I now know you were right. I was foolish and more than a little selfish myself. You'd just lost your sister. Your whole family was grieving. Yet I asked you to leave them." He balled his hand into a fist and tapped at the chair's arm as if to reinforce what he said. "And you were right. We would've broken up. We were too young. We lived too far away. Even if we were just friends, things probably would've fizzled out—maybe badly. And my dad…well…he had his own ideas about my future."

"I thought so."

"Really?"

"Well, you'd mentioned it, and frankly, I got a similar talking-to from my parents, especially after you left." The nights of crying came back to me with such force I was sure I'd weep again. My voice croaked. "After you left, I missed you so much."

"Nicki, like I told you, I missed you, too," he said, tilting my head to his.

"But now…"

"No buts. If we dwell on all the obstacles between us, we'll never get anywhere." He tucked an errant strand of hair behind my ear. "Maybe we had to be apart all those years so we could be together now."

"Adam…" I wasn't sure what to say, and really, all I wanted to do was sob. The tears welled in my eyes. I couldn't hold them back any longer.

He used his thumb to gently wipe away my tears. "I can't have you crying, Nicki. You're going to make me start, and blokes aren't supposed to."

That was like an invitation to bawl, and the tears spilled out of me. Like he wanted to stop the bleeding, he kissed my cheeks, but my blubbering didn't cease. In what felt like a last-ditch effort, his mouth was on mine, giving me the most passionate of kisses. We made out through my tears, though it didn't feel sexual to me. Passionate yes, but not a hormonal rush. I was too much of a mess.

Eventually, I broke away and snuggled beside him. He stroked my hair, still trying to comfort me, but I was emotionally spent. Closing my eyes, I found some peace.

It was only when David knocked on the glass door that I saw Adam had fallen asleep as well. "Adam? It's late," David said. "We should get going."

"Right. Yeah. Be there soon." He was totally groggy.

I propped myself on my arm and blinked at the light shining from inside. "We must've slept for a while."

"It's past three," he said, checking my watch.

"Sorry." I giggled.

"Don't be. It was nice." He touched my cheek. "You probably have to work tomorrow."

"I do."

"I do, too."

"You don't usually work that much on the weekends."

"I know. I try not to." He sighed. "But I'm leaving on Wednesday to see my dad."

"How's he doing?"

His expression alone told me it was bad. "My mum won't say much. I don't think he's responding to the treatment as well as we hoped he would, so I'm going to see for myself."

"I'm sorry. I'll call you when you're there." I kissed his cheek and smiled. "I'll try not to call too late."

"I'll stay up for a phone call from you. Maybe we can get together when I get back."

"Well, I'd like to see you again." I tried to find the right thing to say but couldn't, so I made an understatement. "Tonight was…good."

"It was very good," he said and leaned in for another kiss.

Chapter Eleven

As my conversations with Adam became more frequent and longer, my talks with Juan Carlos became more infrequent and shorter. Phone sex was a thing of the past. I held things back from him, and I was pretty certain he was doing the same with me. Was he seeing someone else?

The idea of him going out to dinner with another woman, even flirting with her, was fine. I could even handle a kiss. Imagining him doing anything more made me jealous, but not in a rage like I felt about Adam and Felicity. Instead, my jealousy over Juan Carlos was sad and full of regret because it was my own damn fault.

Yet I couldn't give up on Adam. I felt like I had to play it out or I'd never feel right about any guy, whether it be Juan Carlos or Adam or someone else. Plus, my time with Adam was so damn fun, I didn't want to stop seeing him.

Our conversations changed, though, when he was back in Cambridge that week. The moment he picked up my call, I heard the exhaustion in his greeting, but it seemed more than just a physical drain he was experiencing. I could hear his bed creak as he answered the phone, and I envisioned him lying down. "Just the person I want to talk to right now," he said with a sigh.

"Aw, thanks. I know you're probably seriously jetlagged. I called as early as I could."

"I told you I'd wait up for a call from you." A few seconds lapsed, and he said, "I've missed you."

"I've missed you, too." I grinned, though no one else could see it. "How are things?"

"Not so good."

"Tell me."

It was like he'd held everything in since he'd gotten home. Sylvia had visited recently but hadn't informed him how sick his father was. Her parents had told her she didn't have to stay, so she'd left early. Adam was pissed with her and his parents, though I'm sure he was madder at the cancer than anyone. She'd wanted Adam to see it for himself. As for his mother, she was around his father twenty-four-seven. Apparently, she was oddly at peace about his decline, like she'd been coming to terms with it for quite a while.

When he seemed to run out of steam, I asked, "Is your dad still eating?"

"Yes. Why?"

"Well, I just remember with my grandmother that she was doing okay until she stopped eating. I think both she and her body decided they couldn't fight the cancer any longer. I don't know if that's true for everyone, but maybe it's something you could look out for."

"Oh. Okay." He yawned into the phone. "Sorry about that. So do you think I can go back to DC? Or should I stay here in case he gets worse?"

"I don't know, and I really don't know your family very well. But if Sylvia thought she should leave, you might want to do the same."

"But why wouldn't he want his children here? We're a close family. It still doesn't make sense to me that Dad only wants us to visit—not stay."

"Like I said, I don't know about your dad. But I'm pretty sure one of the reasons my grandmother liked having me around was that it spared my dad from having to see her so sick."

"Hmm," he said, mulling it over. "That sort of makes sense. My father is so goddamn private as well. Maybe there's something to that."

"Just a thought." I let out a dark chuckle. "I'm kind of good with the death thing."

"I must say you are. I'm sorry you've had to go through it, but I do appreciate your insight."

"Thanks. Happy to help," I said, feeling warm and fuzzy. After all the times Adam had been there for me, it was nice to return the favor.

We talked each night that he was in Cambridge, and while the conversation did have a lot of gloom and doom, there was also work talk and plenty of lighthearted moments of sexual innuendo. His final night, he didn't have long to speak because he had to leave early in the morning to get to London and then fly back to DC. He was surprisingly formal when we said goodbye.

"Thank you for calling every evening."

"What?" I laughed. "Don't thank me. I love talking with you." As soon as the words came out, I knew I'd said the wrong thing. I did not need to be throwing "love" around, even if it wasn't in the I-love-you context. I blurted out my goodbye. "Well, I gotta run. Catch up with you when you get back. Night." Then I quickly hung up.

I stared at the phone, now regretting hanging up more than what I'd said. It was so childish, but I wasn't about to call him back. Then a text popped up on my screen.

You didn't let me say goodbye. Goodnight, Sweetheart.

I leaned in to read the screen again. There it was. *Oh my God. He called me sweetheart.* That had been his name for me in high school. Of course, it was a common endearment and he probably said it to every woman he'd ever slept with, but to me it still felt special.

Not wanting to ruin the moment, I typed a simple response.

:) Goodnight.

The next weekend, DC was in the middle of a spring heat wave. Sylvia was in town, and we made plans that she'd join Adam, David, Lisa, and me for dinner Saturday night. With the heat, though, David decided we needed to be outside, and he and Lisa came up with the idea to go canoeing on the Potomac.

We all met up at the boat rental place. Four of us looked like we were ready for a hot day on the river's muddy water — we were in swimsuits, shorts, and T-shirts. One of us — Sylvia — looked like she was heading off for a day yachting in the Mediterranean.

"You look great," I said, giving her a hug. "Very resort-like."

"Sylvia thinks we're in the south of France, so she traded in her usual black for white," Adam commented with some brotherly annoyance.

"It reflects the sun," she said in a huff as she smoothed out the fine linen of her caftan, but to me, she was kind. "Thank you, Nicki. You look great as well."

"Yes, you do." Adam touched my ponytail and planted a swift kiss on my cheek.

"Thanks," I said, pleased with the kiss. "It's good to see you."

Adam smiled and twirled my hair for a moment. He seemed to be thinking something that I was sure I wanted to hear, but David interrupted the scene when he placed his hands on Lisa's shoulders and declared, "And how is my lovely princess? Are you ready for me to take you on a ride?"

From the way he'd said "ride," it was pretty obvious what he was really talking about. When she shook her head, he rubbed her shoulders. "Come on, love. It would be the ride of your life."

"Oh God," Adam muttered and took a drink from his water bottle. Sylvia turned her back on her cousin and looked at her phone. I couldn't help but watch the spectacle.

"My life is just fine," Lisa said, jabbing him in the side with her elbow.

"But you've never been on this boat." David laughed.

"Your *princess* has been on enough boats to know better," she said. I could tell she was trying to be tough because her lips turned up into a slight smile. "I told you that."

I glanced at Adam and Sylvia, who were still uninterested in David's routine, and tried to change the topic. "Uh, David." I chuckled. "Lisa was the coxswain on the Columbia crew team. She's been on quite a few boats."

"Brilliant. That means she knows her way around…a boat," he said.

"Yes," said Lisa. "And it means either I'm rowing the boat today or I'll be shouting orders at you."

He raised an eyebrow. "I like a woman who tells me what to do."

"Yeah, right." She lowered her baseball cap over her eyes. "Let's just get the damn boat, and we'll see who should row."

Adam wrapped his arm around my shoulders and pointed to the canoes. "Come on. Let's take Sylvia on her cruise."

When we got on the water, Sylvia did look like she was a passenger on a ship while Adam and I were the deck hands. Leaning back at the boat's bow, she wore a giant hat and equally large sunglasses. As Adam rowed, she took in the scenery and spent half the time chatting with us and the other half making phone calls to her new boyfriend in New York.

It was still a great day to be out on the water. Adam and I talked about work for most of the time, and occasionally we'd hear Lisa barking orders at David in their canoe. After an hour or so, she announced, "David, you're a lousy boatman."

"Well, love, I promise you I'm very good at other things."

"All men say that, and it's not true." She laughed.

Leaning closer to Adam so she wouldn't hear me, I said, "You know, she's not this mean to other guys."

Adam snickered. "I think David knows that. It's what keeps him going."

Then Sylvia yelled from our boat, "David, what in bloody hell are you doing?"

"David, sit down!" Lisa cried out.

"But I thought we might swap places," he said as he teetered along, attempting to walk across the canoe.

"David," Adam shouted. "That's not how you do it!"

And with that, David capsized their boat. Flailing about in the water, both Lisa and David laughed, even when she was shrieking at him. To his credit, he quickly righted their boat, and both were back inside in only minutes.

As soon as he got in the canoe, David took off his wet shirt and sat in his swimming trunks. With his wet hair and glistening body, he looked even better than at the soccer game. My eyes widened when Lisa also took off her T-shirt and revealed a very skimpy bikini. She really was being a tease.

When David grinned, she chided, "You tipped the boat just so I'd take off my clothes."

"Maybe." He pointed to her. "Though I'd say by the size of that bikini you don't mind me looking. And you do look good, love."

Lisa smiled begrudgingly. "I'd say the same to you, but I think you hear it enough."

"Not from you."

"You know, this is the second time you've stripped in front of me."

"I hope it's not the last, princess."

As I watched their conversation, I was a little jealous. First of all, they were wet. While I didn't necessarily want to go into the gross Potomac, I was hot in my one-piece and clothes. If I weren't with Adam, I'd have probably taken off my T-shirt by now, but it seemed too forward to strip, especially with Sylvia completely covered in her white caftan.

But I was also envious of how freely Lisa and David talked about sex. All their tension was out in the open, whereas mine with Adam was all bottled up. Yeah, we had some sexy banter occasionally, but I was definitely holding back, and I knew he was as well.

I glanced over at Adam and saw him staring at me. I wondered what he was thinking, and when he gave me a sly smile, I knew. He grumbled under his breath, "I really wish my sister wasn't on this damn ruddy boat."

"I heard that, Adam," Sylvia called out while I looked away.

When we made our way back to the shore, Sylvia announced she would cook dinner for us back at Adam's.

Lisa came up to me and said, "I need some dry clothes, so I'll head home. David's going to come with me. Do you want anything?"

David and Lisa alone in our apartment? That meant only one thing. He'd finally worn her down. I smiled. "Bring me a change of clothes, okay?"

When we got to Adam's apartment, the place was hot from shut windows and no air-conditioning. He suggested we all take showers, and Sylvia insisted I use the guest bathroom first while she started cooking. With her waiting in the kitchen, I kept my shower short.

I couldn't bear to put my stinky swimsuit back on afterward, so I decided to go commando until Lisa showed up with my clothes. Adam was still in his room when Sylvia and I exchanged places. She told me not to touch a thing in the kitchen, so I first quickly texted Lisa to ask for a pair of underwear, too. Then I was left alone in Adam's apartment with nothing to do. I spied his bookcase and went over to investigate.

The giant shelves held books and all sorts of mementos, photos, and art. In the far right corner, higher than I would normally look, a small print caught my eye. I had to stand on my tiptoes to reach it, but as I got closer, I recognized the sketch. I knew it well because it was a famous one in Houston's Menil Collection, a place I'd been to a hundred times. That particular print was even more familiar to me, though—I'd given it to him.

Oh my God. He still has it. I gingerly took it off the shelf. Tracing around its edges, I smiled as I saw he'd even kept it in the cheap metal frame I'd bought. I hadn't known any better at that time.

As pleased as I was that he still had the piece, I didn't want to be caught being too nosy. I rose again to return it when I noticed a book that had been behind it. It was an ancient-looking collection of Wordsworth, so I exchanged the print for the book.

As I admired the aged cover, Adam walked in. "Hello," he said, walking slowly toward me. He looked and smelled fresh, making me smile.

"Hi. Sylvia is in the shower." I held up the book, running my hand along the leather binding. "This is beautiful. It looks very old."

"It was my grandfather's," he said as he came to my side.

"Really? That's wonderful." I remembered how much he'd loved his grandfather. I opened up the book and saw there was something in it. "What do you keep in here?"

He didn't answer, but he didn't need to. I had already lifted out the photograph of me taken almost sixteen years before. I looked so young, sitting on the beach with the Gulf of Mexico behind me. I glanced down at the open page just to see if there was any significance to where he'd placed it. Recognizing the stanza immediately, I swallowed hard and whispered, "'Splendour in the grass.'"

It could've been corny, but it wasn't. That poem was depressing; our history was too sad for it to be sentimental.

Like he'd been caught red-handed, Adam exhaled hard. Without reading the book, he recited the Wordsworth that was so fitting for us.

> *"What though the radiance which was once so bright*
> *Be now for ever taken from my sight,*
> *Though nothing can bring back the hour*
> *Of splendour in the grass, of glory in the flower;*
> *We will grieve not, rather find*
> *Strength in what remains behind."*

The moment was significant, but I wasn't quite sure why. Was it because he'd kept that photo for all these years? Or because he still felt the same way today?

I simply said, "Yeah, I know it. I was an English major."

He nodded, and I looked back down at the photo. Touching a corner, I added, "That was a long time ago."

"Not so long ago."

I lifted my eyes to see him staring me down. After a few seconds that felt like an eternity, I had no sooner placed the book back on the shelf when he grabbed me in his arms, and our mouths opened up to one another. It was a good thing he kissed me, because I couldn't have stood to look at him any longer. My emotions were helter-skelter, and kissing him gave me something to do and a way to convey them. As he moved his lips over mine with abandon, however, I felt like something had snapped for him, but what?

After a moment, I gasped out the same question I'd asked him months ago on the dance floor: "Adam, what are you doing?"

Through a rush of kisses, he murmured, "I'm falling in love with you again."

Savoring what he said, I kissed him harder. He may have only been falling right now, but I'd never had control with him. Since we'd met again, it had been a steady descent for me. Reason left me altogether because I felt the same way, but was I ready to acknowledge it aloud? That would change everything. Instead, I acted like a guy and said all I could with my body. Weaving my fingers into his hair, I pressed against him as we kissed. In only a moment, I found him hard against me.

As much as I wanted him, I held back as best I could. "We can't," I said.

"We can." His voice was firm, kissing me along my neck.

"But no…"

"But yes." He pulled away and put his hands on my cheeks. It was an endearing action, but his expression was sober. "I love you, Nicki, and it's not simply that you're an old flame. This is new." When my mouth dropped open in shock, he then smiled reassuringly and said, "I love you, and as long as you know it, I don't care who else does."

Could I be as brave as him? I wasn't sure, but the moment called out for me to be just as honest. I wrapped my hands around both of his fists and slowly pulled his hands off my face. With a beaming smile, I stood on my toes to get closer to eye-level with him and declared, "I love you. I think I always have."

He nodded toward the Wordsworth on the shelf. "Well, you can see a part of me never stopped."

Just then Sylvia called from behind, "Adam, you left me no hot water. The shower was freezing."

Adam winced like I'd seen him do so many times over his sister. He sighed and said quietly to me, "Obviously, this isn't the end of our conversation."

"I hope not," I said.

Sylvia had caught us, because soon after I heard her footsteps, she blurted, "I'm sorry. Pardon me. I didn't mean to interrupt."

"Well, you did," Adam said.

"Sylvia, let me help you cook," I said and headed for the kitchen.

While we cooked, Adam sat on a stool, drinking beer and keeping us company. Occasionally he and I would look at each other and smile. It was that same giddy feeling all over again. I couldn't believe it.

After several unreturned texts and calls and almost two hours later, David and Lisa arrived — their hair still very wet. As I took my change of clothes from Lisa, I said to her out of earshot, "You look like you just got out of the shower. What were you doing all this time?"

"We took a shower together," she said, fiddling with a stack of napkins on the counter. "That's it."

"That's it?" I snorted.

"Yes," she replied, still not meeting my eye.

"Who takes a shower together and doesn't have sex?"

Before Lisa could respond, David handed her a glass of wine. "Here you go, love."

David kept us laughing throughout dinner, which went on for hours. Afterward, we sat outside on Adam's patio, talking and drinking — except for me. I fell asleep on Adam's shoulder. When I woke up, everyone said it was time to call it a night.

As the others walked inside, Adam pulled me back into his arms and kissed my hair. "Stay here. With me."

"I think Lisa wants to leave now." I ran my fingertips over his handsome brow. "I should go inside."

"No. I mean spend the night with me."

"I can't, Adam." Spending the night together was a nonstarter. That was tempting disaster just a bit too much.

"Tomorrow? Can I see you tomorrow, then?"

"Yes, but it has to be late. I've got to work. You know…big trip this week." The president had his first visit to the UK and then a NATO meeting in Istanbul. I'd be slammed.

"Of course," he said. "I'm flying out a day early to see my dad." He tousled my hair. "So I'll come over at nine in the evening, then."

"Great." Though I worried he might think tomorrow he was spending the night, I pushed that thought aside. I wanted to hear him say something one more time, and he did.

Tipping my chin up, he kissed me, and somewhere during our long embrace, he reminded me, "I love you."

I grinned. "I love you, too."

Lisa and I didn't talk much as we drove back to the apartment that night. Most likely, she feared a further investigation of her time with David, and I was completely preoccupied. My brain tingled with happiness over Adam. I didn't want to be distracted from that giddy feeling, nor was I ready to share it with her yet. The whole I-love-you thing was a major milestone that had a lot of impacts. I wanted some time just to relish it before I had to make any life decisions. If I told Lisa about it, she'd go straight to the decision-making, and that was going to suck.

But my little la la land was interrupted by Juan Carlos shortly after we arrived home. When I saw my phone flash his name, I checked the clock. It was past one in the morning, but he was in Honolulu, six hours behind. He'd been there for over a week, supposedly work-ing for a Senate candidate, but I was pretty sure he was spending an equal amount of time at the beach.

I picked up the phone. "*Hola.*"

"*Hola, preciosa.*"

That was the first sign something was up. As our relationship break had grown into a strained separation, I'd stopped hearing little terms of endearment from him. I sort of missed hearing him call me those sweet things, but I also knew I didn't deserve them. So now having him call me gorgeous put me on red alert. He *shouldn't* be saying those things to me. What was going on?

"How are you?" I asked.

"Great. It's awesome here."

"Because it's Hawaii."

"It reminds me of home—of Cuba. It's made me think. We should come here together," he said eagerly. That statement alone caused me to panic, but when he added, "In fact, can you get away this week while I'm still here?" I knew something had changed with him.

I kept my response measured, though. I didn't want to have a big blow-up on the phone, and I hadn't even really processed what had happened between Adam and me that night. I needed to buy some time. Thankfully, I had an easy excuse. "I wish, but I'm heading to Europe this week."

"Ah, that's right. Okay. Next vacation, then."

So now we were back to planning vacations together? While I didn't want to hash things out with him yet, I needed to know what was up. "Well, you sound chipper. What's been going on?"

"I've been thinking, *mi reina*. We need to start fresh. Take some time together, just the two of us. I bet things will be back to normal, even better maybe, if we do it."

I clutched my stomach, feeling a little ill. Yes, the conversation was uncomfortable for me, but the thought of being on a romantic vacation with Juan Carlos hit me in the gut as...*wrong. Just plain wrong.*

I forced a smile on my face so that it might come through in my tone as I said, "How about we start with dinner after I get back from Europe?"

"That's a start, but I was thinking more of a vacation."

"You know a vacation isn't possible for me right now."

"I know." He chuckled. "I respect your work, but you'll eventually need a different job if we're going to make those babies together."

I scowled. Telling me to quit my dream job was not the way to my heart. "The same could be said about your work. Remember that."

"Now, don't be upset. I was just saying. That's off in the future." The bass in his voice became stronger as he said, "We're at a different stage right now, and I miss you."

"I miss you." I cringed after I said it. I did miss him, but not in the same way. I realized I had to get off the phone before saying outright lies. "Gosh, I just saw the time. I have an early morning meeting tomorrow. I need to get some sleep."

"An early morning meeting on a Sunday?"

"Yeah." So maybe the meeting was actually at eleven, but that was early to some people.

"I'm not finished yet, *preciosa*." Sex oozed from his voice. "Why don't you just lie back on your bed? *Quiero desnudarte con mi voz.*"

Holy shit. I jolted upright hearing the dirty talk. I couldn't have phone sex with him. It wasn't revolting, but it felt completely wrong and dishonest. Worse, though, was the feeling I'd be betraying Adam. Before he could say anything else, I flat out lied to him. "Oh hell. Matt is calling me. Something must've happened. I need to go."

"Goddamn it," he muttered and then sighed. "That's important, though. Go take the call."

"Thanks." I needed to add something else, but I couldn't honestly say, *"I love you."* And I didn't want to say I'd talk again that week. Instead, I pushed everything off and in rapid-fire said, "Ack. The line is beeping. I'll plan that dinner for next week and get back to you. Good night."

"Good night, *preciosa*. I—"

I killed the line. I didn't want him to say, *"I love you"* either.

Chapter Twelve

The following night, Adam came over right on time, and it was only seconds after I shut the door that he wrapped his arms around me for a long kiss. I was happy to oblige, but afterward I laughed. "This is quite a hello."

"I thought I'd try some nonverbal communication."

"Very funny."

"I think we're good at it."

"We sort of learned together, didn't we?" I asked a little bashfully.

"We did." He nodded toward the living room. "Where's Lisa?"

"In her room. On the phone with David." I smiled. "I swear I might've heard her giggle, but I know she's still toying with him."

"She's playing him perfectly, as far as I can tell."

"Come on," I said, tugging his hand. "Let's have a beer."

After some awkward conversation in the kitchen, he suggested we go back out onto the balcony. As soon as we got out there, he led me to the chaise lounge again.

"I thought we were going to finish our conversation from last night," I said.

"Maybe we should continue our nonverbal communication." He sat down, pulling me into his arms.

"Adam…"

His mouth was on mine before I could finish. For a few minutes, I thought, *What the hell.* I love the guy. Why couldn't I make out with him? As things progressed, though, I realized he was just getting started. He was there to have sex, and *that* I wasn't ready for, no matter how much I wanted it.

"I love you," I said after I broke our kiss. "But I need to slow down."

"I don't want to slow down." His lips searched for mine again.

"But I need time." My tone was insistent, which caused him to freeze for a moment.

He eyed me suspiciously and said, "You know I'll resign tomorrow if it will make you feel better."

"That's sweet." I gave him a half-hearted smile. We were back to his silver-bullet solution, as if I hadn't had a boyfriend or a life before he'd come along. "But it doesn't change—"

"And I don't care if you have a reputation for sleeping with the press." He poked my side.

"Oh, that's fine for you to say," I said with a touch of derision.

"In fact, I'd like for you to have a reputation for sleeping with me." His eyes were sparkling with playfulness, but his expression became more deadpan when he added, "As my wife."

"What?" My mouth gaped open, and I jolted up from his chest. He had to be joking. "Adam, I—"

"There." His tone became all seriousness, but he touched my cheek. "I've put my cards on the table. I love you."

"I…I love you, too. But I don't know if I'm ready for this. I don't know if you're ready for it."

"Well, I am ready. I'm bloody sure of it."

"Are you?" My skepticism filled the air.

"I rang Felicity this morning. Told her we needed to talk when I was in London this week. I'm going to break things off permanently."

"Oh…"

"What about Juan Carlos?"

There was no way I was going there. I'd tried to forget about last night's call, so I simply held up my hands as if I was helpless.

Adam stared me down. "Well, seventeen years since we first met, I'm certain." He gulped, and his confident demeanor changed as he qualified himself. "But I think you're not certain about me."

Shaking my head, I gently touched his temple. "I'm certain I love you."

I hadn't meant for it to be a pledge, just statement of how I felt. But he evidently took it as more as he grinned and leaned down to kiss me. I had to awkwardly look away and began fidgeting with my watch. "But we loved each other before, and look how that turned out."

"Aw fuck, Nicki. *That's* what's holding you back? Me messing around with Kate." He sat up and hit the arm of the chair with his fist. "I'm sorry I broke your heart, but you'd broken mine. I was seventeen and a scared, hurt idiot. It's history, and that's not me anymore. I want to be with you and only you."

"This is all new…" My dilemma was dizzying. It was one thing to feel love for someone. It was quite another to change your life for them, and that was what he was asking me to do. I began to babble, "I need time, and this is a bad week for me, and—"

"Well, I don't need time, and it's not all new. On one level or another, I've known this for half my bloody life. It sounds like you may have as well, otherwise you wouldn't have avoided me for a decade and a half."

"But right now isn't a good time—"

"Bollocks. It's never going to be a good time. We just have to make it happen." His lip curled in annoyance. "If you don't see that, you're not as clever as I thought you were."

Now that pissed me off. I glared at him. Maybe he could take or leave his job, but I had so much more to lose than he did. Couldn't he see that? "Given the situation, I think I'm acting very intelligently."

"Maybe acting intelligently, but not smart."

I looked away for a moment, wondering what had become of the kind man I'd been with just the day before. Why had he turned into this demanding asshole? What was his deal? I again fidgeted with my watch, fully expecting to hear an apology from him in just a few seconds. Instead, I heard him say, "Come with me to see my dad. Come home with me."

"What?" My head jerked up.

"Just as I said. I want you to come to Cambridge with me. I'd like for you to see my dad before…well, before. It's important."

"Adam, I want to be there for you, but you know I can't do that." It was a snap judgment, but I thought it made sense. I was going to

London for work. I didn't need to be traipsing all over England to see a dying man who never really liked me, especially when things were so uncertain with his son.

But what I thought was a sensible decision Adam took as an insult. "Well, why the fuck not?"

"Because."

"Because what?"

This time he slammed his fist against the chair so hard the sound made me jump. Hoping to calm him down, I said slowly, "Give me some time. I'm thinking it through…"

"Goddamn it, Nicki." He shook his head in exasperation, gently pushed me aside, and climbed off the lounge. When he stood up, his eyes were fixed on me as he demanded, "Then think. Think about why you won't. What else is holding you back? Juan Carlos? You don't love him. If you did, you wouldn't be here with me. Is it your job? It's just a fucking job. I'll tell you, in the grand scheme of things, whatever it is, it's not important. You're what's most important to me. And from what you've said, I'm important to you. So let's stop pissing around and get the fuck on with our lives."

I had no idea how to react to what he'd said. I was utterly confused.

When he saw that I wasn't giving him immediate feedback, he took another swig of beer and then said, "You know how to reach me. I'm leaving for the UK on Thursday." Then, abandoning me on the balcony, he said, "Good night."

As usual, work was my refuge from my personal life for the next few days. Work made sense. The men in my life did not, so I focused on what I could do well. The one day I saw Adam at work before he left for London, he thankfully ignored me. Then he never called me at all, and I was too annoyed and admittedly a little scared to call him. I also avoided Juan Carlos. I let all of his calls go to voicemail and answered with a short text, telling him I'd see him the next week.

But I couldn't escape Lisa, and she could tell I was in a funk. She cornered me in the kitchen the night before my trip. "What in the hell is going on with you?" she asked after I didn't respond to her simple question about dinner.

"Just a lot on my mind from work."

"Come on. There's something else. David asked what was up, because Adam has been a bear to be around."

The jig was up. Squinting as I felt the pain again, I said, "Adam sort of gave me an ultimatum and walked out on me."

"Did he now?"

"Yes."

"Well, it took him long enough."

"What does that mean?"

"Nothing."

"It's not like I've been leading him on. He knows exactly where things have stood with Juan Carlos, and he's been with Felicity the entire time. Supposedly, he's breaking up with her when he's in London."

"But you still won't commit?"

Lisa was pissing me off. She'd always been the rational one of my friends, the one who'd been skeptical of Adam back in high school because he was an unknown. Any reasonable person should've seen *now* what I'd be giving up if I took it any further with him.

I threw my hands on my hips and said, "I've got a lot to lose."

"Is this about your job?"

"In part."

"Because I'll tell you what one of my med school professors told me, and it's the damn truth. She said she never heard anyone on their deathbed say they wished they'd spent more time in the office."

"My job isn't just *any* job."

"Everybody says that."

I tried my other argument. "But you *like* Juan Carlos."

"He's a good guy, and he'll be even better with another woman." Her hard veneer quickly vanished, and she placed a hand on my arm. "We've known each other a long time. I've never seen you happier than when you're with Adam, back then and now. Do you really want to lose him again? Think about it," she said and left the room.

I always slept with my phone's ringer on, just in case there was an emergency at work. At one in the morning, I heard the buzz faintly through my sleep. Blinking at the bright screen, I saw the call was from Matt.

"Hey," I said, propping myself up on my arm. "What's up?"

"Sorry to call late, but I thought you should know before you get questions from the entire White House Press Corps on the plane."

"What's going on?"

"I was up checking the *Washington Post* for a story, and I happened to see a headline with your name in it."

"Oh my God." I slapped a hand to my heart in terror. *How did anyone find out about Adam and me?*

"Do you know what I'm calling about?"

"No." I grimaced at my lie and the reprimand I was about to receive.

"If you don't know already," he said with a chuckle, "I'm happy to be the one to tell you that Juan Carlos was seen looking at engagement rings in Tiffany's yesterday. It's a blurb on *The Reliable Source* blog."

I exhaled a breath of relief. Matt wasn't calling to chew me out for causing a political crisis for the president on the eve of a big trip.

Then the fear came back, only more mildly. *Shit. Damn Latin guy.* For once I rued that Juan Carlos was Cuban. Of course he would run off and do something over the top to get me back, like surprise me with an engagement ring. I imagined him presenting me with it, and the vision forced an answer out of me. It was like my heart silently called out, *But I don't want to marry him.*

I placed a hand over my eyes, like shielding them would lessen my problems. When I remembered I must give Matt a believable response, I pretended to laugh. "Thanks, Matt. What are you going to say when they ask you about it?"

"No. What are *you* going to say when they ask you about it?"

"Probably that I don't respond to gossip columns. Of course I'm not going to tell them anything!" It was both a handy and honest response.

"Well, the White House doesn't comment on the personal lives of the president or his staff."

"Great. Thanks for calling. I really appreciate it. Let's both get some sleep."

"Huh." He was quiet for a second. "That's it? I thought you'd be overjoyed."

"I'm just too tired."

"I guess so," he said, clearly on to me. "We can talk tomorrow. Good night."

I ended the call and tossed my phone on the nightstand. There was barely any sleep for me for the rest of the night. At any moment, I was sure Juan Carlos would call with a proposal, and I had no idea what to say.

When I got out of the shower the next morning, I saw the light blinking on my phone. Still in my towel, I dripped water on the tile as I listened to Juan Carlos's message.

"Morning, mi reina. *I'm sure you've heard by now. Just so you know, I hate the press."* He then laughed at his own joke and said, *"No need to return the call. I know you're leaving, and I don't want to talk to you on the phone anyway. I'll see you when you get back. Have a safe trip. I love you."*

I'd dodged a bullet. Thank God he wanted to propose in person. I quickly typed him a text.

Screw the press (don't quote me on that).
You still surprised me. Love you.

Before I hit send, I stared at the last part. Did I mean it? What would he think? I decided those two words really didn't matter. They could mean a lot of things, including absolutely nothing.

The following morning in London, I arrived at Number Ten Downing Street ahead of President Logan and his entourage. My staff and I tried to shoo away some of the crazy tabloid photographers by promising them an extra photo-op just for them later that day with the First Lady. As I talked to various paparazzi and my counterpart on the British prime minister's staff, I would occasionally catch a glimpse of a man who had to be Adam, though I wouldn't look long enough to see. Most of the White House Press Corps hadn't shown up yet, but Adam must've been there early since he'd been on London time for a few extra days.

I wondered how he was doing. The last update I'd heard on his father's health had been last week, and the prognosis hadn't been good. How was Adam handling it? Was he lurking around trying to talk to me? I felt a pang as I realized that, in my heart, I hoped he was.

But the pang morphed into a deep gut wrench when the next logical question hit me. Adam was back in London now. Had he seen Felicity? Had he broken it off, or had all my dithering made him decide he wanted to stay with her? I wanted to throw up just thinking about it. I was in the thick of work, though. I couldn't have an emotional breakdown at Number Ten Downing Street. I may have been crazy, but I wasn't insane. Straightening my suit jacket, I blocked the thought and asked one of the British staffers a stupid protocol question just to dive back into my job.

Later, as the prime minister and president took questions together at their joint press conference, Adam was in the best location at the front of the press gaggle. I had a great view of him, but he couldn't see me. Still, I tried not to stare. I looked everywhere I could to avoid him, surely making me appear very distracted.

When it came time for the two leaders to pose for photos, the room erupted with the noise and glare of mass photography. Matt leaned down and whispered in my ear, "You keep scanning the room. What are you looking for?"

"Nothing."

"You look exhausted."

I sneered. "So do you."

"Touché." He smiled. "Thinking about the wedding?"

I flinched so hard Matt stepped back. He stopped smiling and went from nosy-boss to big-brother mode. "It's okay. I won't ask about it again."

"Thanks."

I nervously smoothed my hair, which I'd pulled up into a bun. If Matt thought I looked exhausted, I must've looked like shit. Plus, I was an emotional mess, crying off and on for the last few days. I let my eyes wander one more time over to Adam, and this time I saw he was eyeing me, though his eyes revealed no intent. He only gave me a blank stare before quickly turning away. It was the kind of look you might give someone you either despised or simply had no opinion of whatsoever because they were so inconsequential to you. And now Adam had felt the need to look at me that way.

My brow furrowed, and I frowned. Maybe I didn't need the guy to be in love with me, maybe I could live with him being with Felicity or some other bimbo, but I couldn't stand him hating me. While the light of flash bulbs filled the room and reporters shouted additional questions to the president, I finally accepted Adam actually *had* been my friend all along. You cared what a friend thought of you.

The fact was, Adam had been there for me as I grieved for Lauren. He'd been there when I was seventeen, and he'd even let me cry on his shoulder now. And what had I done? I'd rejected him when he had asked me to come with him to see his dying father. I was a shitty person. I wouldn't want me as a friend either.

After the car accident, I'd learned to deal with pain—emotional, physical, and that which intertwined the two. For purely emotional pain, I'd stuff it away in tidy boxes, and over time, I'd usually get enough courage to unpack it all, sort through it, and move on. Physical pain was another matter. I endured it immediately, rolling along with the agony. I just knew Adam was rejecting me, and it created a combination of pain there was no packing away.

Waves of hurt slammed into my heart as I made my way through the day. Adam's words from the weekend haunted me. I'd seen him angry with me once before. This time he was infuriated, but the theme was the same: I was being cruelly selfish simply to avoid potential anguish.

When I finally made it to my hotel room late that afternoon, I shut the door and dove into my bed. I threw a pillow over my head, recounting what he'd said on Sunday, but that scene got mixed with the old one in my mind. It was like he'd re-infected an old wound.

"But we could be friends. And you never know what's going to happen in the future," Adam said.

In a total panic, I sputtered, "I can't do that. I can't watch our relationship die a slow death. I think we should break up when you leave." I gulped in air before my finale. "I don't think we were meant to be. I think this is it."

"Are you mad? You think that because we've got…geography problems, that we should just split up?"

Nodding, I started to cry. "I think it would be easier."

"That's complete bollocks. How long have you been thinking about this?"

"A few weeks." I started bawling, and my feelings tumbled out of me. "I can't do it, Adam. It's too much. It will be easier for me if you just leave. If I don't have to talk to you when things are impossible between us, it will hurt, but not for so long."

His eyes narrowed at me. I'd never seen him so upset. "I can't believe I have to say this to you, Nicki, but you're being fucking selfish as hell. This solution may be easier for you—although I doubt it is—but it would be hell for me. There are two people in this relationship, not just you."

Reliving that moment made me cry all the tears again. The last time I'd rejected him, I had pushed him into the arms of Kate. Was it going to be Felicity this time? Or would anyone be better than me?

Chapter Thirteen

A little after nine that night, I stood on the porch of what looked to be a stately brick house. After a deep breath, I rang the doorbell, which chimed loudly both inside and out of the house. A moment of silence passed, and then I heard shoes patter toward the door.

When the door opened, a handsome woman in her sixties studied me quizzically. She looked familiar to me. Did I look familiar to her?

"Well, hello there!" She reached out for my hand. "Nicki, this is such a wonderful surprise."

"Good evening, Mrs. Kincaid. I apologize for the late hour. It's the soonest I could get away."

"But of course." She grinned. "I believe there was a state dinner tonight you probably attended. It's lovely for you to visit regardless of the time. Do come in." As I crossed the threshold, she called down the hallway, "Adam, stop with the dishes. Come here!"

I smiled, fighting knots in my stomach that were the most nervous of my life.

She turned back to me. "I want you to know how impressed we are with you. It's such fun watching you on television."

"Thank you. That's nice to hear."

Down the short hall, Adam appeared, no longer in his suit from the morning but now in jeans with a dishtowel thrown over his shoulder.

His mother turned to him. "Adam, you didn't tell me Nicki was coming."

Our eyes met, and he smiled. Staring at me, he replied to her, "I didn't know if she would."

"I'm sorry I'm so late." The trip to Cambridge was so impulsive I really hadn't planned out what I might say. Repeatedly apologizing for being late seemed liked a safe thing to do.

He took the dishtowel off his shoulder and placed it on a side table. Taking both of my hands in his, he kissed my cheek. "Better late than never. Thanks for coming, sweetheart."

He'd called me sweetheart again; maybe I was forgiven. "I'm happy to be here." And I truly was. He released my hands, but I slipped my right one back into his left. This time, I didn't want to let go.

When I looked over at his mother, I saw she'd been watching every one of our moves. She sputtered, "Oh. Yes. I should tell Dad that Nicki is here. He's probably still awake watching the telly."

As she hurried down the hall, Adam turned back to me and grinned. "Thank you for coming."

"I wanted to." If only I could've thought of something more eloquent to say.

"You look tired."

I'd known I looked like shit, and now he confirmed it. I grumbled, "It's been a hard week."

"You and me both," he said, squeezing my hand.

Then Adam's mother called from the hallway, "Adam, your father is awake, and he'd love to talk to you, Nicki."

Still holding my hand, Adam led me through the tasteful living room and down a dimly lit hall. I noticed there were scads of family photos lining the walls. I slowed down so I could examine each one.

After a moment, Adam tugged on my arm. "If you really must see photos of me on my first day of nursery school wearing school shorts, I'm sure Mum can show them to you later."

I laughed. "I'd like that."

When we entered the bedroom, his father was in bed under the covers, wearing pajamas and a robe. The television was on but muted. He greeted me at once with a cheery, "Nicki! Good evening."

"Good evening, Professor Kincaid." I approached him and shook his hand. "Thank you for seeing me this late."

"Not at all." He smiled and shook my hand more enthusiastically than I'd expected. "It's so kind of you to come all the way out here. I'm sorry we couldn't visit you while you're in London."

"Oh, it was an easy trip for me." Nodding toward the hall, I added, "And this way I got to see some old photos of Adam."

"Ah, yes. I'm sure he loved that." He smiled at his son, to which Adam gave a half-hearted eye roll. His father then gestured to the armchair by his bed. "Nicki, please sit here with me for a while. I'd love to hear about your work."

Adam's dad was a brilliant man who happened to be bedridden and watching television all the time, so he was more up-to-date on current events than many and had more insightful opinions than some of my staff. The conversation was enjoyable, even when he started lobbying me to get Logan to increase federal funding for science. After only a few minutes, Adam's mom called for him to come to the kitchen.

Adam shook his head. "No, I'll stay here with you two."

"Go on, Adam. See what your mum needs," said Professor Kincaid.

"But…er…" Adam shuffled, clearly not liking the idea of leaving me alone with his dad.

"It's okay," I said with a reassuring smile. "I'll keep your father company."

"All right," he said, giving his father a wary eye. "I'll be back in a minute."

Being alone with Adam's father was fine because he was so chatty. I'd forgotten how interesting he was and felt sort of bad for having been so negative about him all these years. Yes, he was a snob, but in the end he hadn't wanted his seventeen-year-old son to go nuts over a foreign girl when the relationship would only fail. My parents had said the same thing, and I'd ended up agreeing with them.

I only became uncomfortable when I saw the signs of his decline. It wasn't the room's smell or his skinny hands or his jaundiced skin that bothered me. It was the thought of what those things were doing to Adam.

It was much longer than a minute before Adam returned. His mother must've kept him busy. When he walked back in, his father was still speaking, but his eyelids had begun to droop. I'd been listening patiently as he went on about different places he'd been in the United States. I smiled at Adam and then placed my hand on his father's arm. "Oh, I'm sorry to interrupt, Professor Kincaid, but Adam is back. I should get going if I'm going to catch that last train."

He fought to fully open his eyes. Not quite achieving it, he reached for my hand again. "Yes. You should. Thank you for coming, dear. It's been nice to catch up with you."

"I feel the same way. Thanks for having me. This was the most fun I've had all day. Good night."

"Such a pleasant girl," he said in his rambling way. "Take good care of my boy."

My heart stopped for a moment. What did that mean? Then again, dying people could say such crazy things. "Of course I will," I answered.

"Nicki, I'll take you to the railway station," Adam said, his voice a little tight.

I smiled at him again, hoping it would make him feel more comfortable. As awkward as the situation was for me, it had to be worse for Adam. But his expression warmed as he gazed at me. He took a few steps to be at my side and placed a hand on my shoulder.

His father smiled, too, withdrew his hand from mine, and closed his eyes before saying, "Good night, you two."

Adam led me out of the room, and he took my hand in his before we walked out the door. As much as I wanted to be with him at that moment, I knew he should spend as much time as he could with his family. "You know you don't have to drive me. I can take a cab."

"Ridiculous. I'll give you a lift."

As his mother and I said goodbye, she told me she'd love to see me the next time she visited Adam in DC. I offered a tour of the White House, which made her a little giddy. Adam then drove me to the train in his dad's ancient yet immaculately kept Mercedes. I took charge of the conversation, asking him question after question about Cambridge. I was interested, but I was mainly trying to keep it light.

When we pulled up to the station, he said, "You have a few minutes. Please don't leave yet."

"I won't."

He turned off the car but then said nothing. If I attempted more light conversation, it would sound silly. So I simply said, "I'm sorry about your dad. This is so hard for you."

His forehead wrinkled, and he touched the steering wheel. "It is hard."

"Oh, Adam," I said, reaching over. I rubbed the short hairs on the nape of his neck, and he leaned back into my hand in silence, closing his eyes.

After a few seconds, he opened them and said matter-of-factly, "He's declined. A lot. He's barely eating, and the jaundice is awful. It probably won't be too long."

"No, it probably won't." My instinct was to comfort him, so without thinking I kissed his forehead. "This won't make it better, but I'm sorry."

He smiled but then pulled back from me and looked me straight in the eye. "Why did you come here, Nicki?"

"I came for you."

"That doesn't tell me much."

"Maybe you're not listening." I leaned over and, through a breathy kiss, said, "I love you, Adam."

"I love you." He grinned. "Thanks again for coming."

"Thanks for asking me." My eyes darted to my watch. I was dying to know about Felicity, but I wouldn't have enough time to approach the subject tactfully. And on second thought, it felt tacky. Adam had just welcomed me into his home. I shouldn't be interrogating him, no matter how jealous I was. "I need to run. Istanbul in the morning, you know."

"Take care. I'll see you in the morning on the plane."

He leaned in for what I thought would be a peck, but he kissed me full on and hard, with a hand sneaking between my legs. Was he going to feel me up in the middle of a parking lot? I kissed him another moment because it felt so good, but then I warned, "Adam…"

"The tease doesn't like being teased, does she?"

I giggled and shook my head. Wherever things stood with Felicity, I felt like the front-runner again. After a swift kiss on his cheek, I bolted out the door. "See you tomorrow."

Chapter Fourteen

As I sat on the train back from Cambridge to London, the planning began. I'd been lying to too many people, including myself, for too long. It was time to come clean, but how and when and in what sequence? There were too many impacted by my actions, including the friggin' president of the United States. I was already in trouble. I needed to do things correctly or I'd make it all even worse. Checking my calendar, I saw this trip lasted two more days before we were back in the States, so I had forty-eight hours to do no more damage and figure out what to say to whom and when. Was Juan Carlos first? Then Logan? Or Logan and then Matt and then Juan Carlos? I wasn't sure, and I wanted to do this by myself. It would be best if Adam wasn't involved in the disclosure.

The next day we flew to Istanbul, and after marathon meetings, I hoped to spend the night holed up in my hotel room. It was too bad because Istanbul was a beautiful city, but getting my life together was more important. Matt, however, had other plans. Buoyant from Logan's successful NATO talks that day, he suggested we join the press corps for their night on the town. I declined.

"Come on, Nicole," he said with hands in the air. "It's not every night you get to drink in a Muslim country. You need to have some fun."

"I need some sleep. That's what I need. And people drink here, you know. We're in Turkey, not Saudi Arabia."

"That sounds like a good enough reason to celebrate. Come out and enjoy Turkey's secular society." He tapped his watch. "Meet me in the hotel lobby at eight."

Later that night, Matt and I walked to the restaurant together, but I couldn't even enjoy the stroll through the city. While he commented on the Blue Mosque's wonderful architecture and said hi to all the shop owners standing at their doors, I was engrossed in my own little world, wondering if Adam would be calling me later or if I'd see him at the table. We hadn't talked since he'd left me at the railway station; our only communication had been a smile and a wink. A night out with the press corps wasn't really Adam's style, though, so I assumed I'd just give him a call when I was back in the room in an hour.

When we arrived at the restaurant, reporters and White House staff had filled a couple of fifteen-foot-long tables. Adam, to my surprise, was there sitting between two German journalists. He smiled at me, and I could hear enough from the conversation that they were debating the last European soccer championship. I looked for an open spot not far away, but Dan Roark waved me over to him.

"I heard you were coming out, Johnson." He nodded to the empty seat next to him. "I saved a seat for you."

I smiled. *Shit.* I shot Matt a look. This was not going to be fun. Matt smirked and found a chair nearby. When I glanced at Adam, he gave Dan an annoyed sneer, but there was really nothing I could do about it. I had to sit with the guy and make small talk. I shouldn't have worried, though, because Matt was at the table. Everyone hung on his every word, so I didn't have to talk too much to Dan.

Things changed after dinner. The restaurant was part traditional Turkish café, part cheesy disco. Soon after our meal, the DJ cranked up the music, and some people got up to dance to a bizarre mix of music. Matt called over to me to say that he was leaving, and I made a move to leave as well.

Dan stopped me. "No way, Johnson. We haven't gotten to talk yet."

"I'm really tired, Dan. I'm sorry."

"Come on…how many times do you get to dance to Air Supply in Istanbul?"

Lydia Mixon also chimed in. "Please stay, Nicole. It will be fun."

I really wanted to go back to my hotel room, but a bunch of reporters wanting to hang with me was an opportunity. In a few days,

I was about to create a professional shit storm, so it was probably a good idea to be on their good side. While I said that I would stay, Adam caught my eye, and as soon as there was an opening, he moved over to my table. Was he really so jealous of Dan Roark?

It wasn't long before I realized why they were so intent on keeping me there. They all wanted to ask about Juan Carlos and if we were engaged. Granted, some of them had already asked over the last few days, and I'd always tell them I don't comment on my personal life. Now all the women at the table were going on about weddings.

I watched as Dan nodded to Lydia right before she casually said to me, "So, Nicole, if we should believe *The Washington Post*, I think you've got some news for us."

Dan leaned back in his chair and snickered. "Yeah, that's right. *The Reliable Source* mentioned Juan Carlos at Tiffany's. Should I offer you my congratulations?"

I gave my usual perfunctory smile when I addressed questions from the media that I really didn't want to. I needed to walk a fine line. I couldn't lie, given what was about to happen, but I also didn't want to say too much. I turned the subject back on them. "How do you know what he was buying or who it was for?"

"Well, we don't," said Lydia. "But you do. Please, Nicole. Are you engaged?"

"No," I said with a shrug. "He hasn't asked me."

"Are you going to say yes?" asked Dan.

"Why on earth would I tell you?" I laughed and glanced at Adam, who didn't look pleased.

"That's a good enough answer for me. You're still single at the moment." He rose from his chair and said, "How about we dance?"

I kept a smile frozen on my face the entire time Dan and I danced to a smarmy love song. No doubt because he thought he had a chance with me, he didn't inquire any more into Juan Carlos. He did go on and on about the ski house in Jackson Hole he planned on buying once he got an extra million added to his new contract with ABC. When I didn't say much in return, he asked, "You ski, right?"

"Not at all. I grew up in Texas."

"Tell me about Texas," he said, his hand wandering a little too low on my back. He hadn't touched my rear, but the way he danced with me was very possessive. I wanted out of there, and just as I was about to plead to call it a night, Adam was at our side.

"May I?" he said to me and not Dan.

"Sure." I smiled, though I was anything but happy. Why was Adam calling attention to us?

"I see I've got some competition," Dan said in irritation.

"No competition at all, mate," said Adam. He could be such a cocky bastard sometimes.

Dan skulked off while the DJ made a uniquely Turkish segue from Maroon Five to Frank Sinatra. I smiled—not for Adam, but for whoever might be watching us. "What are you doing?" I said in a tone that didn't match my smile.

"Dancing with you."

"Adam…"

"If you can dance with that arsehole in front of everyone, you can dance with me."

"But it means something when I dance with you."

He peered over my head at our table. "They can't tell."

"But I can."

"I can, too." His smiled vanished. "So old Juan Carlos has bought you a ring. We haven't talked about *that* yet."

"No, we haven't. Apparently he's purchased it, but it's true that he hasn't proposed. He's waiting until I get back."

"And does he have reason to believe you'll say yes?" He then smirked. "Or *si* in this instance?"

"Don't be silly." I shook my head. "I had no knowledge he was doing this. It's some weird last-ditch, grandiose gesture to get us back on track."

"Latin tosser."

"Huh?" There was that word again. "Is that some British cricket term? What does this have to do with sports anyway?"

"Never mind." He chuckled. Clearly, I hadn't found the proper definition yet. He smiled and swirled me about the dance floor. "Start at the beginning, then. What's been going on with you?"

"Well, when you stormed out on me last Sunday night, I was angry. I'd been trying really hard to do the right thing and be fair to everyone—to you, to Juan Carlos, to my job—and you gave me no credit for it. I wasn't happy, though after thinking things through, I have to say you made some valid points."

"I suppose you're right. You've been quite fair in what is a very hard situation." With a quick squeeze of my waist, he added, "Except for when you haven't been able to control yourself around me. That's been a little unfair. You've been drinking tonight. I hope you can keep your hands to yourself."

"You're horrible," I said, suppressing a smile.

"Only because I adore you." He chuckled.

"And I you."

"So you'll get rid of JC?"

"I can't just 'get rid' of him, Adam. This is a little more delicate than that."

"Shit, Nicki, when are you going to make a choice?"

"I've made my choice. It's you. Don't you see that?"

"Then when are you going to act on it, damn it?"

"Act on it? I am! I'm trying to do things in order. It's not like—"

"It's not that difficult. Don't you see that I'll do whatever it takes to make things work between us? Hell, I've already broken up with Felicity."

"I don't think your situation with *Lady Fucking Felicity* is the same."

"Oh, really? Given the row we had when I ended things, she might disagree."

As the Sinatra song ended, I huffed. "We should go back to the table. This isn't a good place to talk. Let's do it when we're back in DC."

He wouldn't let me go, though. He gripped my hand more tightly as the DJ made another random turn to Roberta Flack's "Killing Me Softly." Leaning closer to me, he whispered, "Don't go. I'm sorry. One more song."

I glanced around the room and saw a table full of very curious White House reporters. Adam was so insistent, though, I rejected my better judgment and stepped a bit closer to him.

His tone changed to a smooth one. "I promise not to complain."

"Oh, all right," I said, pretending to be put out. "There are worse things than dancing with you."

"Like what?"

"Dancing with Dan Roark."

"I swear, I hate that wanker. I don't like seeing him with you."

"You say I don't listen to you. Do you listen to me? There's no way I'd ever be with that guy — or any other guy, for that matter."

"Well, maybe we should both listen and not talk." He caressed my hand in his.

"Okay."

After that, neither of us said anything, which turned out to be a bad idea. The silence made us all the more present. As we danced, we kept getting closer and closer to each other. It was like our bodies were taking care of all the years of pent-up emotional and physical frustration between us. The sad lyrics of the song hung in the air, and at one point, I accidentally rested my cheek against his chest.

When he laid his chin on my forehead, I jolted from the embrace and then froze. "We can't do this here. We have to stop."

"It's okay, Nicki."

"No, it's not." I released his hand. "Let's talk tomorrow…when we're back in DC."

When I arrived at the table, I saw that Dan was leading the group in a round of shots. "That was a long dance," he said, raising his shot glass to me and then Adam.

Dan seemed suspicious, as was probably the whole table. There was only one thing to do: prove I was loaded and flirting with everyone. "I'll have a shot, Dan."

"Great," he said, as if I'd chosen him over Adam. "Here you go."

Placing some Turkish lira on the table, Adam said, "No need to pour one for me. I'm heading off." He then said a formal goodbye to me and every other woman at the table.

As he walked away, Dan pushed a glass to me. "Let's see if Nicole can hold her liquor."

I got drunk — wasted, in fact — though most of the press at the table just thought I was really giggly. Dan kept flirting and ordering me drinks, and I kept accepting them to make up for rejecting his passes.

After midnight, Lydia made sure I got to my hotel room okay, and when I locked the door behind me, I sank onto the floor. The cool tile felt like the most comfortable place on earth, so I grabbed my phone, lay down, and scrolled through my messages. There were voicemails from Juan Carlos to ignore, boring work emails to read, and a text from Adam.

Call me when you get back to your room.

I frowned. A heavy conversation was the last thing I needed. I tried to get my wits by focusing on the bad art on the wall across from me, and as it blurred in my sight, I realized while I might not have wanted to talk to Adam, I did want to see him. For a split second, I remembered him placing his hand between my thighs the night before, and then all sorts of sexy Adam memories came back to me.

What if... I thought. *No.* That was a terrible idea. I'd spent all this time being meticulous about how we were seen and how I would tell everyone about us. *I can't just go sleep with him. If I do that, we could get caught.*

I stretched against the wall, feeling horny as hell with no release. I glanced at the clock and considered my idea again. Adam would be elated if I snuck into his room. We'd probably have the shag of our lives, as Adam would say, and at that late of an hour, if I was careful, no one would ever have to know. I needed information and an alibi, though, so after a moment I made one up and called the front desk. The clueless graveyard shift concierge was happy to provide Adam Kincaid's room number so a White House official could hand-deliver an important document to him.

Five minutes later, I looked around the dead hallway and knocked on Adam's room.

"Who is it?" he called from behind the door.

I said nothing, and when he cracked the door open, his shocked face met my smile. I slipped inside, and he shut the door with a laugh. "Well, good evening. This is a nice surprise."

I kept quiet as I walked into his room, which was nicer than mine.

"What's all this about?" he asked, coming toward me. He was only wearing plaid boxer shorts, and he looked sexier than anyone had a right to. My raging hormones approved.

"What did you say earlier? 'Why wasn't I acting on it?' You said something like that, I think."

"I did."

"Well, I'm here to act on it." I met him halfway and kissed him hard and fast. In case he didn't quite get the purpose of my visit, I found his dick and began tickling it over his boxers.

He exhaled at once. "Fuck…"

"Yes," I said, practically hissing. I greedily slid my hand into the flap of his boxers and found what I'd been hoping for. His penis was hard, but his foreskin was soft and ready to be played with. "Let's go to your bed," I murmured.

"Gladly."

He led me over to the bed, but I surprised him by pushing him onto it. He laughed as he fell. "Assertive, aren't we?"

"A little." I smiled as I said it, simultaneously kicking off my heels.

He lay on his back, resting on his elbows, and watched my quick strip show. Beneath my conservative work clothes, I'd always worn great lingerie. It was sort of one of my secrets to remind myself I had a life outside of work. Today, the lingerie came in very handy as I stripped out of my suit pants, exposing a very racy black thong. Adam smiled, though his focus was on my crotch. He was eyeing me so lustfully, I ended the strip show early.

I leaned toward him and tugged his boxers down. His dick was so perfect, I had to give it a kiss and a few licks, but I soon moved on. I was a woman on a mission. Sliding off my panties, I straddled him. His eyes were set on his dick, and he rubbed the head of it against me. When I moaned, he said, "God, you're beautiful."

"Do you like watching me do this?" I asked.

"Fuck, yes."

"I love the feel of you against my pussy."

He smiled warily. *Oops.* He was probably unsure what to make of me, because seventeen-year-old Nicki had never said anything like that during sex. My year with a dirty-talking Cuban was showing through to my proper British boy. It was time to cut the conversation anyway. I gave him such a forceful kiss he was flat on his back while I continued rubbing myself against him.

His hands reached down to my ass, and I said, "I want to feel you inside of me. Now."

"Uh…"

Poor Adam seemed at a loss for what was happening. I still hadn't even taken off my shirt. It wasn't how I'd imagined our reunion sex would be either, but it felt right, and it definitely felt good. "Please," I said.

He mumbled something about a condom, but I said I was on the pill. Then he mentioned taking my shirt off. I was too eager to finally feel him to go through that whole rigmarole, so I simply lifted up the front tails so we could both see as I slowly slipped his erection inside of me.

Adam and me together again was bliss—hot, blinding bliss. I sighed, and our eyes met.

"At last," I said.

"At last."

That was the extent of the romance of our second "first" time—then we fucked. It wasn't long, but it was intense. We both ended up a panting, spent mess. As we calmed down lying on pillows, I traced circles onto his chest and he nuzzled into my hair.

"I love you, Nicki."

"I love you." I raised my head to give him a smile, and he quickly took the opportunity to kiss me. I was a little surprised that he was ready to go again, but if he was game, so was I.

He slowed it down this time and began to unbutton my shirt. When he discovered my lacy bra, he groaned. "I always loved your breasts." And he went to work sucking and nipping and groping—all of which made me feel more wanted by him than I ever had.

My appreciative whines and moans urged him on more, though, as he began to move southward on my body. At first, I was excited at the thought he was going to go down on me, but then I saw what he was doing. He had stopped at the scars on my torso, tracing one of the silvery feathers that marred my skin. And then he did just as he always had—he kissed them, each and every one.

The eroticism of the moment vanished. As he brushed my scarred body with kisses, I could only think of how long it had been since he'd done it and how I had been sure he'd never do it again.

Whenever I was drunk, there wasn't a lot of nuance to my emotions. They were always strong and demanded to be seen. If I was turned on, I wanted to have sex then and there. If I was happy, I wanted to giggle and giggle. And if I was sad, I wanted to bawl. So as I thought back to the times when I'd been certain I'd never see Adam again, tears came quickly, and I couldn't stop them. They started as a quiet roll but only gained momentum as I relived my time without him.

After a minute of me quietly crying, Adam raised his head, confused by the sounds I had started to make. I let myself sob, gasping my breaths. "I missed you…I missed you so much. For years, I missed you."

He crawled back up to my side at once. Placing a hand on my cheek, he said, "Nicki, I will never leave you again. Never. But you have to stay with me. Okay?"

I nodded and eventually smiled through my tears. "I'll stay with you…always."

Chapter Fifteen

A headache, thumping away at my temples, woke me up. I winced at the pain and discovered I was nauseated as well, and then I realized where I was. My head spun around to the clock radio on the hotel nightstand. Four thirty in the morning had never looked so good to me. I could still get out of there without anyone seeing me. Even the most dedicated person wanting coffee or a workout wouldn't be up at four thirty.

I made sure not to wake Adam as I quickly slid out of bed and found my clothes. Buttoning my shirt, I studied my sweet man as he slept. His features were so chiseled, but he looked like a little boy with his face crammed against the pillow. I hated leaving him like this, but I knew if I woke him up, I'd get delayed, and time was something I didn't have enough of.

As soon as I was dressed, I grabbed the hotel pen and paper and scribbled:

> Adam,
> I'm sorry I have to leave early.
> I'll talk to you after I get everything lined up on my end.
> I love you,
> NICKI

Speeding out of the room, I wondered if he would understand what I'd written. He was a reporter; I hoped he would see that I'd clearly meant, "Don't call me. I'll call you." We may have danced across some ethical lines before, but after last night, we had obliterated the professional division between us. I had to clean up the mess—and now.

As I slinked down the empty hallway to my room, I talked myself out of re-imagining my worst nightmares. No one knew about my night with Adam. The worst they knew was that we'd gotten a little too close on the dance floor, that I'd then flirted with Dan Roark as well, and that I had been so drunk, Lydia Mixon had walked me to my room.

I simply needed to initiate the plan I'd already hatched. The only difference now was that I had to do it ASAP, and Juan Carlos wouldn't be the first to know.

No one crossed Melba McCutchins. She was a formidable woman, and as the personal secretary to President James Logan since his early lawyering days, she was as close to him as family. Even the prime minister of Britain didn't get on the president's calendar without her approving it.

I'd known her for a long time, and yet I was in no better place with her than any other staffer. No matter how many times she called you "sugar" and "honey," she was still a little scary. Rejection did that to you, since more often than not her answer was usually no, and if you objected, it was "Hell no."

As soon as I could get to her that morning, I did. We had some meetings at the embassy before heading back home, and I found her working away in an empty junior ambassador's office.

She peered at me over her bifocals. "Good morning. What can I do for you, hon?"

"Morning, Melba." I put on my strongest smile and phrased my request as a demand rather than a question—because, really, there wasn't a question to be had. *I must talk to Logan.* "I need to get on the president's schedule for five minutes before we arrive home today."

"Sorry. That's impossible." She went back to her laptop. "I'm sure you can catch him for a minute after the press conference."

"I need more than a minute, and it must be private."

Slowly raising her head from her computer, she took off her glasses. "Excuse me?"

"It's important."

"May I have an idea what this is about?"

I shook my head. "No. Trust me. I wouldn't be making this request if I didn't have to, and I know when something rises to this level of sensitivity. I need scheduled time alone with the president."

"Why isn't Matt coming to me about this?"

"I'm sure the president will bring Matt in shortly after we meet."

She bit on the end of her glasses in thought. "Are you resigning to get married?"

"I'm sorry, Melba, but I'm just not telling you anything else, except that it's more than a minor personnel issue. I know you'll keep that confidential."

She bit down on her frames a few more times before saying, "Because this is coming from you, I'll say yes."

"Thank you." I exhaled. "I truly appreciate it."

Returning her attention to her laptop, she said, "You'll get five minutes on Air Force One before his nap." She smiled. "The Cubs are on. Maybe he'll stay up."

When it came time for me to knock on the door of the president's private quarters on Air Force One, I was rattled. I'd spent much of the day fending off jokes about my drinking the night before. The good news was that word had spread among the press that I'd partied with a few of them and was thus on their good side. The bad news was that rumors had already started that I must not be interested in Juan Carlos if I'd been hitting on two reporters. That really wasn't bad news, though, because the truth would be far worse.

"Come in," Logan boomed from the interior.

I walked inside and immediately smelled popcorn. Closing the door behind me, I saw Logan lounging on the sofa. The Cubs game was on the television, and he had a bowl of popcorn and a beer at his side. I laughed. "I thought you would be resting."

"That's what I'm supposed to be doing." He gestured to the TV. "But the game is on. Sit and join me."

"Thanks," I said, taking a seat. My voice had wavered, and it never wavered around Logan. I'd known him for too long.

He frowned at my nervousness. "Now tell me what's going on. Melba thinks you're resigning because you're getting married. You know you don't have to do that. We'll find you a job with shorter hours."

"I'm probably resigning, but it's not because I'm getting married. For one thing, I'm not marrying Juan Carlos."

"Really? What's going on? I'm sure it's something we can manage without you quitting."

"I…uh."

"Just start at the beginning."

Every time I'd role-played with myself how I would break the news, I had started with a simple declaration of the present facts, like, *"I'm in a romantic relationship with Adam Kincaid of the BBC. One or both of us will resign immediately. I apologize for the problems this is going to cause. I know how serious they are…blah, blah, blah."*

Yet it seemed all wrong now.

"Yes?" he asked impatiently.

As I sat, completely inarticulate and staring at Logan, I realized he would care less about *how* we dealt with the mess. That was easy in the end. He was the president, and he could do whatever he wanted and make whatever needed to happen, happen. Instead, Logan would want to know *why* the mess ever came to be in the first place.

Why? I asked myself. It might've been fate, but that seemed kind of cheesy to tell the commander in chief, and I still wasn't sold on the idea of fate anyway. Lisa would say there was an underlying cause and effect that had brought Adam and me back together. In my heart, I knew what it was. We'd gotten back together because the ties from our past were too strong to ignore.

Logan wanted the story from the beginning, but the beginning of us didn't start in January when we'd both begun our jobs. The beginning started long ago.

I bit on my lip in determination. "You know that my sister died in a car accident, right?"

"Well, yes." He muted the television entirely. I must've gotten his attention. "It's a tragedy few would forget."

"Right. It was awful."

"I remember when your dad and I worked at the firm together and, in the usual water-cooler conversations, he would mention you. Often someone would ask if you were his only child, and he'd always say, 'Actually, I have another daughter, Lauren, but she died a few years ago.' He wasn't trying to make the person feel bad. I think he just liked the opportunity to talk about her in the present tense."

That made me smile and gave me a shot of courage. "So I'm going to tell you a story that starts the year she died."

"Go on," he said in his fatherly way. "I'm all ears."

After a deep breath, my life spilled out of me. I tried to be as forthcoming as possible, and Logan prodded me along, asking questions all the way. His face was placid and his questions as objective as if I were relaying a policy issue to him. There were none of the curse words or bulging neck veins that came out when he was angry. His detached demeanor was actually helpful to me as I finally confessed my feelings for Adam to someone else.

When I finished, I said, "So that's it. Full disclosure. You know everything. As I said, I did inform Matt that Adam and I had a relationship in high school, but I didn't give any details." I gulped because it was like I was letting down my boss and my dad at the same time. "I'm sorry for that."

Logan was quiet for a moment, pressing his fingertips together in thought. It was a pose most commonly used when he chose policy positions or dealt with political problems. And now that was me. One big political liability that had to be addressed.

When he finally spoke, his tone was flat, and his expression continued to be void of emotion. "As your boss, I must say you made a mistake—a serious one. I'm disappointed in you for that. But as a friend, I can see why you made the decisions you did, though I respect and like Juan Carlos. It's a shame you did this to him. Does your father know?"

"Almost nothing."

He shook his head. "My kids wouldn't have told me either."

That small show of humanity made me grovel. "I'm so, so sorry, Mr. President. You know this isn't like me. If Adam and I didn't have this history, I would never do something like this."

"You and Adam must have a powerful connection."

"We do."

He took a swig of beer and pursed his lips. "I'm going to think about this. Please go get Matt. We'll come up with a plan."

That was it? I was motionless, expecting something more, but he went back to watching the game, which signaled I was to immediately follow his orders. As I left the room, the whole experience reminded me that you didn't get to be president of the United States being a hot head. They were always looking down the road at every implication—like master chess players, plotting ten moves ahead, while you were still debating your next one. When it came to his job, Logan was emotionless. That could work for me or against me.

Not knowing where I stood with Logan terrified me as I searched for Matt. When I found him, he was asleep in an empty row of seats. I had to rouse him, which made me even more apprehensive.

"What?" he said grumpily.

"The president," I answered, getting to the point.

He blinked a few times and shot up from his seat. "I'm on my way."

As I followed him, he asked, "You, too?"

"Oh yes." I was grim. I'd screwed up big time.

After we settled in the president's quarters, I had no idea what Logan was going to say, but I knew I no longer could talk. He was the president, and it was his moment. His words carried that same impassive tone as he started off the conversation. "We have a problem to manage. It can be done if everyone acts quickly once we're on the ground."

Leaning forward in his seat, Matt was ready to get down to business. "What's the issue?"

Logan nodded to me. "Nicole will tell you."

I couldn't tell Matt what I'd relayed to Logan. It was too personal. So Matt received the version of the story I'd originally intended. I disclosed everything from the time Adam and I had first talked in the White House briefing room, but I didn't tell him anything earlier. I loved Matt as my friend and colleague, but that time of my life was private.

"I'm sorry that I led you astray when I initially told you about Adam and me," I said at the end of it. "It wasn't right."

"No, it wasn't." Matt adjusted in his seat, then chuckled. "Though I should've known when you said you hadn't told Juan Carlos."

"Yeah," I said, not finding it quite as funny. "That was a sign."

No one said a word for a few seconds, and Logan turned to me and gave a puzzled look. He then reached across the sofa and placed his hand on my leg. I hadn't noticed that I'd been nervously bouncing it up and down so hard.

"I'm sorry," I said again, but that didn't seem like enough. I sputtered out another plea. "I'm sorry for everything."

"I know, and I accept your apology," he said kindly as he withdrew his hand.

Twelve hours later, I was with Juan Carlos, telling him the same story, only with less detail. Personal experience had taught me that when you're cheated on, you don't want too much information. You need enough to sort out the why of it all, but any more than that and you create unnecessary pain.

We sat on very uncomfortable sofas in his friend's apartment in Eastern Market. I'd wanted to have the meeting somewhere Juan Carlos could throw me out if he wanted. He deserved that opportunity. Fortunately, his buddy was away on business, so we were alone.

As I relayed the events, Juan Carlos vacillated between icy and annoyed—from making offensive jokes about me being a slut or Adam having a small British dick, to being passionately angry and close to tears as he paced and yelled in Spanish, throwing things across the room.

At the end, I said, "I loved you, still do in a way. I'm very sorry I just didn't love you enough."

"Uch." He held his hand up as if he were the guy on the Heisman Trophy. "Don't. You disgust me. I can't believe I bought you an engagement ring."

"Honestly, I don't know why you did either. It's not like we were ready for it."

That misstep just pissed him off more. He practically snarled, "Well, I was."

"I'm really, really sorry, Juan Carlos. *Lo siento de corazón.*"

"Adam Kincaid. Typical English effeminate asshole. I bet that Felicity chick was just a lie."

"She's not. She may even be a problem."

"Good. You deserve it," he said with a pout.

Seeing the conversation degenerate, I said, "Well, you've now heard how Logan wants this to play out. Please just go along with the plan."

"Logan might have a plan here, but you realize you could be the downfall of a presidency."

I scowled. "I think that's a little overdramatic."

"Maybe, but there could be a congressional investigation."

"Get real. This is a political/PR scandal. No laws were broken."

"I'm glad you can be so flip about it."

"I'm not being flippant. I know it's a big deal. I informed Matt and have now disclosed everything to the president. He thinks he'll be okay."

"Regardless, you've given the Republicans and late-night shows material for weeks." He glared at me. "You've made yourself the butt of jokes and dragged me into it."

"I know. I really can't apologize enough."

"Hmpf." He quieted for a moment before he shook his head and grabbed the remote control on the side table. Throwing it across the room, he yelled, "You deceived me!"

"I did, and I'm incredibly sorry for that." I fiddled with the button on my coat, which I hadn't even bothered to take off. "I don't care what you say about me in the press."

"Oh, come on…" He waved me off. "Like I'm saying a word? A single word? I don't want to hurt Logan, and I don't want to draw attention to the fact I've been a chump. *Me humillaste.*"

That was a verbal slap across my face. I had humiliated him, and I knew what that embarrassment was like. Yet though I felt for him, I couldn't comfort him. My touch and encouragement were the last things he wanted.

Standing up to leave, I said, "Still. You can have surrogates, your friends, talk off the record. Say what you want. Accuse me of whatever. I've probably done it, and for that, I'm truly sorry."

Chapter Sixteen

It wasn't until late that night that I was able to ring Adam's doorbell. When he opened the door, he was just as surprised as when I'd shown up at his hotel room the night before. I'd ignored him all day and hadn't told him I was coming by. I knew I looked like shit, but it wasn't like I'd had any time to myself that day. I smiled and sighed. "Hi."

Leaning against the doorjamb, he cocked a head to the side. "So have you come to shag me senseless, tell me you love me, and then abandon me again? That seems to be your M.O."

"Very, very funny." I placed my hand on his chest and pushed my way inside.

After closing the door behind us, he pulled me into his arms and laughed. "Well, that is what you did last night—especially the shagging."

"So I was a little forward."

"A little?"

"Okay. Maybe I jumped you." I grinned. "I'd say we both crossed a line."

"We crossed it a few times."

"We did, which is why I had to leave. I—"

His kiss stopped me from saying more, and my body melted into his. After a good minute of earnest snogging, as Adam called it, he mumbled, "So you admit you wantonly seduced me, but you claim you were forced to abandon me?"

"Pardon me," I said and pulled away, "if I had to go tell my boss, the leader of the free world, that I'm fooling around with a member of the press."

"We more than fooled around last night, but let's sit down, and you can tell me what happened." He kissed my forehead. "Can I get you a drink?"

"Considering how much I drank last night, I should say no, but after a day like today, I've got to say yes. I'll have some wine."

"I'll be right back. Please sit down. You look awfully tired."

"I am."

While he poured me a glass of wine and got himself a beer, I went over to the sofa and started going through the messages on my phone. When he returned, he handed me the glass and sat down. "So, you're still working. You didn't get sacked."

"No, believe it or not. They didn't fire me." I laughed.

"Start at the beginning. What did you do this morning?"

"Well, I woke up—hung over. That sucked." I kissed him on the cheek. "But I was with you, so that was nice."

"But you left…"

"I didn't wake you because it was really early, and I had to get back to my hotel room without being seen in the same clothes I wore out the night before. Luckily, I don't think anyone saw me."

"Ah…the Walk of Shame. I forgot about that."

"Yes. Something to be avoided in our situation."

"Indeed." He found my hand and gave it a squeeze. "I should tell you that I got more than one look from my colleagues and also a nasty comment from Dan about our dancing."

"Yeah, I figured as much. I got a lot of comments, too. Oh well. We can't do much about that now."

"No, we can't, so tell me more about this morning."

"After I left you, I got cleaned up, packed, and did some work before I went to talk to Melba to get on Logan's schedule."

"You didn't want to talk to Matthew first?" He gave me a skeptical look. "Or Juan Carlos?"

"I thought about it, but after last night, I decided I needed to just go straight to Logan. He's been like a dad to me for so long. He deserved to hear things first."

"So when did you talk?"

"Not until we were on the plane. Logan thought I was going to resign so I could get married, so I first had to tell him I wasn't marrying Juan Carlos."

"What did he say to that?"

"He was surprised, and then when I hemmed and hawed, he asked that I just tell him everything." I sipped some wine and said sheepishly, "So I told him our story, starting at the very beginning after Lauren died."

"You started back in high school? Really?"

"It seemed easier to tell him that way, and frankly, I think it was more compelling. I said after over fifteen years, we'd found each other again, and over the last few months, we've fallen back in love."

I guessed he liked how I'd portrayed things. Smiling, he mussed my hair and asked, "Well, what did he say?"

"Professionally, he's disappointed in me. I've caused a headache for him. But he's still very fatherly and happy that you and I reconnected. Matthew, on the other hand, was a little pissed and taken aback when he did find out, but not totally surprised."

He grimaced. "I have to say I'm feeling a bit guilty you're taking all this heat."

"Don't feel guilty," I said with a cringe. "But I do have to ask something huge of you. I understand if you don't want to do it. There are other ways out."

"What's that?"

"Logan, Matt, and I talked through our options. Of course, you and I can't be in our current roles together anymore. The fairest option is that you and I both quit our jobs. The problem with that one—and the reason Matt doesn't like it—is that it looks like there was some wrongdoing on our part."

"I can see that." He kissed my hand. "If we're both going to lose our jobs in shame, I'd like to have been shagging at least more than one night."

"Amen to that." I laughed. "But actually, that's why Logan doesn't like the idea either. We really haven't done anything grossly unethical yet."

"So what does he want?"

"Well, honestly, Adam, it looks the best for Logan and makes the most sense if you resign and I stay working at the White House." I hung my head, ashamed I was forcing the end of his career at the BBC. "I'm sorry..."

"Don't be. I already told you I'd resign. I meant it."

"Are you sure?"

"Of course. And their political calculus is correct—I wish I'd thought to argue from that angle before. You keep doing what you're doing, and I move on. When it comes out that we've been dating, people will question the timing, but because you're still in your position, it shows the president has faith that nothing untoward happened between us. No state secrets were released, and I didn't go easy on the administration over something. And if I resign now, our relationship is never an issue in the future. It all makes sense."

"But your career..." I felt like such a shit. Sure, Adam had offered me this sacrifice before, but it would have been on his terms then. Now, his future was being decided for him by the president even though he wasn't a US citizen; regardless of nationality, Adam was like a pawn in a totalitarian state.

"My career? I don't give a fuck. With Dad so ill and...well, when he's gone..." He drank his beer as if to steady himself. "I'm going to need some time off. I'd take compassionate leave regardless."

Placing my hand around the back of his neck, I moved in close to him. "I'm so sorry, Adam. This really isn't good timing, is it?"

"I don't think there's ever good timing for something like this." He pulled me into his arms and kissed my cheek. "But considering that I've got you back, I'd say the timing is as good as it gets."

"I love you," I said with some relief.

"I love you, too." He pulled away and smiled. "So if you talked to them on the plane, why did it take you so long to get here?"

"I figured I owed it to Juan Carlos to let him know immediately. I went to see him."

"You did? What did he say? What did *you* say?"

"I was honest about everything, and he was angry...really angry." I frowned, not wanting to relive the bad scene. "I deserve it—even if he and I were on the outs. I deceived him."

"He must despise me."

"Pretty much." I didn't think I should recount all the insults. "He said something about Felicity being a ruse."

"I assure you, she was not a ruse. She may even be a bloody pain in the arse later, but we'll worry about that when we have to."

"Will she say something?"

He was thoughtful for a moment and took a swig of beer. "Even though we've seen relatively little of each other in the last six months, the break-up didn't go very well. She immediately brought up your name."

"What did you say to that?" I asked in fear.

"I said, 'Nicki and I are close enough friends that I've realized what's missing in our relationship.' That's it."

"Oh, that must not have gone over well."

"No, it didn't. Felicity has never thought herself lacking in any way. To hear otherwise was quite an insult to her."

"Will she talk publicly about you?"

"I don't know. I hope not. Will Juan Carlos?"

"Never. He's too loyal to Logan. If he gossips about me, Logan looks bad. But I also think he'd be too embarrassed by it."

"I'm sorry about that, but overall, what a stroke of luck."

"Yeah, finally."

"I realize things can still go sideways pretty quickly, but right now I think we're doing okay."

"Right now, yes."

"I'm very happy," he said, leaning down for a kiss.

"I'm happy, too," I answered before my lips met his.

As we kissed, I felt some relief come over me and loosened up for the first time all day. Our hands roamed around each other's bodies, and when I felt his erection, he murmured, "Let's go to bed."

"I want to, but I shouldn't." My to-do list reemerged in my mind, causing me to sit up straight. "Shit. I'm not done. I need to tell Lisa… and my dad. Before they hear it anywhere else." I smiled. "But I'll call my mom while I'm on the road this week. For any reservations she may have had at the beginning, I know this news will make her very happy, so I don't have to talk to her immediately."

"That's right. There's another trip."

"We leave tomorrow night, remember?"

"*We* don't leave tomorrow night. Only *you* now."

"No more trips together." I frowned.

"Hardly." He wrapped me in a tight hug. "Many more trips together. Just the two of us, though. No fucking Dan Roark along."

I giggled at that. "Where should we go first?"

In one continuous motion, he stood up and cradled me in his arms. "To my bed, of course."

"Adam, I just said—"

"The night is young. You'll see Lisa soon enough, and your parents can wait until the morning."

"But you haven't resigned yet."

It was such a half-hearted protest that I knew it wouldn't stop him. He continued carrying me back to his bedroom and said, "No, I haven't resigned yet. I'll do so tomorrow morning, but I'll text my boss right now if it finally gets you in my bed."

"No need for that," I said, kissing behind his ear.

When we arrived at his room, our kisses were slow, but we hurriedly shed our clothes, helping each other out while tugging at our own. He pulled away to look at me. I felt like I was being judged, but also admired. "What?" I asked.

Tracing the dip of my waist with his fingertips, he smiled. "You're just as beautiful as before."

I glanced down at my chest and muttered, "Not much going on down there."

"You've got a lot going on down there." He held me close and patted my rear. "This part is great as well. No more insults about someone I love."

That earned him a big kiss. When he grabbed my ass, I kissed him again with a laugh before jumping up and wrapping my legs around him. I could feel his erection right beneath me and asked, "Shall we stand?"

"Why yes, thank you." He kissed me, letting his tongue tease mine, and after a minute, I just about died when he said, "Put me inside of you."

"God, yes." My hand reached down to place him just so.

We ended up against a wall, but it wasn't fast and furious like last time. Instead, he was slow and determined, watching me the entire time, which made me come even harder.

Afterward, we went to the bed, and he curled up next to me, pulling me in tight. I touched his chest hair and smiled. "Nothing's changed…"

"No, it hasn't. Though I do hope I lasted a little longer than before. I remember not doing too well your first time. I believe you lost your virginity in the blink of an eye because I couldn't control myself."

"Neither one of us was good at controlling ourselves back then."

Adam laughed. "Some would say we aren't very good at controlling ourselves now."

For the next hour, we planned out the rest of the week—how he would resign, how I'd tell my parents, and when we would see each other again. His father was doing so poorly, Adam planned on going back to London mid-week, but I wasn't coming back from the president's tour of the West until Saturday.

"Will you come home next week, then?"

"If I'm not working anymore, I should just stay in Cambridge and be with him. Don't you think?"

He was so sad when he spoke that I immediately offered, "Do you want me to fly to see you on Sunday? I could take a few days off."

"You're wonderful," he said, hugging me tightly. "I don't think that's necessary."

"We'll talk this week, though, right?"

"Every day, I hope."

As I got dressed to go home, he frowned as I buckled my belt. "I don't like it," he said.

"What? This belt?"

"No. The fact that you're leaving."

"We just discussed this." I kissed his cheek. "I need to talk to some people, and so do you."

"But when we're both back in DC for good, I won't like that you're not here."

"What do you mean?"

Taking me in his arms, he smiled. "Well, I know we haven't been together again for very long—"

"Like maybe a day." I laughed.

"Yes, but given our history, can't we skip the going-out stage?" He kissed my forehead, whispering, "I know that's where my heart is."

"What do you mean?" I asked, leaning back to assess what he was saying, whether he was about to play the wife card on me again.

"Will you move in with me? For now. As a start…"

I chuckled. At least he'd dialed it back a step. "We haven't even gone on one date, and you want to live together?"

"Yes."

"Let's get through the drama around your resignation and our relationship first. Let's see how that goes."

"And then?"

"I agree we need to make up for lost time," I said with a grin.

Lisa was asleep when I came in that night, so I didn't get to speak with her until the morning. As I told her the whole story, she drank her coffee in silence but wore a self-satisfied smile.

After a while, she finally commented with a sigh. "God, I love being right."

"Whatever."

"I can't take too much credit. I wasn't the only one who called this. Rachel did as soon as she heard about Adam, and naturally David did, too. He said it was just a matter of time."

"Really?"

"Yeah, his take was something like Adam finally had the opportunity to make things right and was determined to do it. Of course, he always refers to Adam as his 'sorry sod of a cousin' or something like that."

I laughed. "How *is* David?"

"He's good." She smiled. "We will never last. We don't want the same things."

"How so?"

"His number one goal right now is to make a lot of money and have a good time, and you know me. I don't care about money, and I'm not looking to be someone's good time."

"True." She didn't care about money, and with a former NBA player as a dad, she'd never need it regardless. Lisa simply wanted the same kind of stable marriage and family as her parents. Still, I was hopeful. "But he could be your good time for a while."

"While I'm in DC," she said with a naughty grin, "he's a nice distraction."

"Or as Rachel would say, he's got a nice distraction."

She winked. "One day we can all compare notes."

Chapter Seventeen

After my talk with Lisa, I waited not so patiently for a call from Adam, jumping at anything remotely unexpected all morning long. Whether it be an unannounced visitor to my office or certain numbers appearing on my phone or emails on my screen, I feared the other shoe would drop at any moment. Adam and I would be exposed, and the shit would hit the fan, but when would it happen?

Adam called me at nine, sounding more chipper than I'd expected. "Are you sure you're still interested in me? I'm just an unemployed bloke now."

"Oh my God. You resigned so quickly."

"Well, my bosses are in London, and they're hours ahead of us. I didn't see any reason not to contact them as soon as I woke up."

"So how did it go?" I asked, my stomach flipping.

"All in all, it went relatively well, but only because I resigned. They asked how long our relationship has been going on, and I said it was relatively recent. They asked about Felicity as well. I was scolded, as could be expected, but since I was quitting, I'd taken away their thunder of sacking me."

"That's true. They don't have much to do now."

"My editor even cracked a joke that the school chums had become a little too chummy."

"It's good they could kid about it."

"They immediately asked if the White House knew, and I said you'd disclosed everything to the president himself."

"What did they say to that?"

"To be honest, I think they were a little surprised. They're not daft, though. They called me the sacrificial lamb for the White House. I didn't quite own up to it."

"So are they releasing a statement?" I feared the BBC would feel the need to take the moral high ground and also make a news splash about it.

"No, they feel exposed as well, like the other press will criticize the BBC for going soft on the US president because of their White House correspondent. They said they'd respond only if asked, saying it was a minor personnel issue that had been dealt with."

"Whew." I felt the urge to wipe my brow, yet guilt soon overpowered my relief. "I'm really sorry this has turned out this way for you."

"But I didn't tell you the most important part."

"What's that?"

"They'll hire me back in another capacity in the future."

"Oh, that's great! Especially because we won't live here forever."

"We won't?"

"Well, I mean, I won't have this job forever, and then in the future…if we were still together we could—"

"We're absolutely going to be together. I was just wondering where we might live other than DC?"

That made me smile. "I don't know. I imagine you would want to spend time back in London. Am I right?"

"You are," he said in eager surprise. "How do you feel about that?"

"I think it would be nice for a while."

"You don't know how happy you make me."

Considering I'd always said I wouldn't move for him before, I supposed it would make him happy, and now it was the least I could do to repay him for resigning for me. "You make me happy, too. I love you."

"I love you." He then sighed. "Things haven't been all good this morning, though. Sylvia called with bad news. Dad isn't doing well at all. I need to go home straight away."

"It's that bad."

"Yes, I must go so I can see him before…"

"I'm so sorry. When are you leaving?"

"This evening. It just depends what flight I can get on at the last minute."

"Would you like me to come, too?" I asked without hesitation.

"No, you don't have to. I'll be okay."

"All you have to do is say so, and I'll be there."

"I know. Really, I'll be fine." He chuckled. "And you already got to talk to him."

"I did. He was very kind."

"So, I guess I need to book a flight. Hmm. Funny. I'm unemployed now and without an assistant. I haven't booked a ticket for myself in years."

"Try Orbitz like the rest of us."

"Maybe I will," he said with some fake attitude.

"I don't think our travel schedules are going to mesh very well. I'm going to be out-of-pocket a lot in the next couple of days. Please keep in close touch because I'll want to come later."

"Later?"

I took a breath and brought up the inevitable. "For the funeral," I replied softly.

It took him a moment to say, "Thank you. Having you there will mean everything to me. I'll be in touch."

"I want to be there."

"Then I'll text you when I land in London. I love you, sweetheart."

"And I love you."

Over the course of the next few days, Adam and I kept in touch as best we could given my travel and the time difference. A number of the reporters noticed he wasn't on our trip out West, and the BBC replacement gave no details as to Adam's status other than that he knew Adam's father was gravely ill. Because he was only a junior stringer and not the permanent replacement, I guessed he didn't know the full story. No doubt the BBC would quietly install their new White House correspondent with little fanfare in order to minimize the attention.

I felt horrible for not being with Adam at such a sad time in his life. Yet our phone calls were lengthy as he relayed all the funny things going on in his house despite the grief. While Mrs. Kincaid and the hospice nurse had become fast friends, Sylvia despised her. The nurse had told her to stop wearing stilettos because the clacking was an annoyance to her father. Sylvia had responded that her father had put up with her for thirty years and would expect nothing less of her. David was in Cambridge as well, taking Adam out drinking every night and watching soccer as much as possible.

During one call, Adam complained that the hospice nurse had taken him aside to warn him his dad might die without him in the room. "So now we're all standing by his bed round-the-clock, but I think that advice was just rubbish. Dad's not going to kick off without us there."

"But why would she say that?"

"Her theory is that people sometimes die alone to lessen the pain for their loved ones. Complete BS, if you ask me."

"I don't know…I could see that happening, or if someone was truly a loner in life." I'd spent enough time around nurses to know they were usually smarter than doctors, at least when it came to stuff like this.

"Do you really think they have a choice for when their body dies?"

"Maybe. We decide when we go to sleep, don't we?"

On Wednesday night, when Adam's father finally passed away, he died with only Adam's mother in the room. Adam was devastated. He cried on the phone with me, making me tear up also. When he'd pulled himself together, I asked, "When is the funeral?"

"Sylvia is in charge. It's a big do on Friday—a memorial service at Trinity College Chapel, but then we'll go to Scotland on Saturday to bury his ashes on the estate Sunday. That ceremony will be small and just family."

"Well…I—"

"Nicki, you don't have to be here on Friday."

"I want to be there. I just need to figure out how."

"Where are you right now, anyway?"

"In Aspen, Colorado. There's a big fundraiser tonight at a swanky house."

"Please, don't cut your trip short. You get back to DC on Friday. If you could make it on Saturday so we could go to Scotland together, that would be wonderful, but, really, that's not necessary either."

"Well, let me see…"

That night at the fundraiser, Matt was in great mood, both from bringing in a haul of cash for the Democratic Congressional Campaign Committee and from the mojitos that had been served. I caught him when he was ordering another.

"Matt, I've got a request that I know you're probably going to turn down."

"What's that?"

"I realize I'm in the professional doghouse for what I've done with Adam, but—"

"But what?" he asked, taking his third drink from the bartender.

"But Adam's dad died this morning, London time."

"That's too bad. Please give him my condolences." He didn't quite pronounce "condolences" correctly due to the rum in his drink.

"I will. If I leave tomorrow, I could make the funeral in Cambridge on Friday."

"So you're asking for a few days off even though we're in the middle of an important trip and, as you said yourself, you're in the doghouse?"

"Yes," I said, feeling the futility of my request.

He took another drink. "Everyone's going to want to know where you've gone off to."

"I know. I know they will. But do you have to tell them I'm at Adam's dad's funeral? Can't you just say I had a personal matter come up?"

"Okay." He took another drink, then his words slurred as he added, "Who's going to see you in Cambridge anyway?"

"Thanks, Matt," I said, touching his arm. "You're the best."

When I made it back to my hotel room that night, I pulled up Orbitz to book my flight, and I texted Adam.

I'm going to try to make it Friday morning. I love you.
I'll be in touch.

Chapter Eighteen

On Friday morning, it was a mad dash for me to get from Heathrow to Cambridge in time for the funeral. That was something I didn't want to show up late for. I'd texted Adam that I'd try, and if it didn't work out, I'd see him at the wake at his house.

It turned out I only had minutes to spare as I arrived at Trinity College Chapel. Adam stood on the steps of the church, shaking the hands of what appeared to be a crowd of Cambridge faculty and upper-crust British society. It dawned on me at that moment that Adam was now the head of the Kincaid family, the brand new Viscount Adam Kincaid. He was going to receive a lot of attention. There was even a photographer lurking around taking photographs of the mourners.

As I paid the private hire driver, I asked him to deliver my bag to the Kincaid's house. Then I hopped out, hoping to catch Adam before he walked into the church. Only the family and a few stragglers remained outside, and the family would walk in last. I hurried toward the chapel, and Adam spotted me.

He walked straight toward me with a grin, and when we were close enough, he grabbed me in his arms and hugged me tightly.

"I made it," I said with a sigh.

"You did." He grinned. "And I love you for it."

We kissed once, then twice, and then a third time. That last one went on for a bit until I pulled away and smiled. "Adam, this isn't the place."

"I don't really fucking care." Then he winked. "And I know Dad doesn't either."

Taking my hand in his, Adam kept it there, locked in place, for most of the service. As we took our seats at the front of the church, he stared straight ahead at the altar. No doubt eyebrows were raised at the unknown brunette walking down the aisle with the Kincaid family. His mother and Sylvia seemed happy to have me, occasionally smiling or patting my shoulder.

The funeral was the traditional Anglican mass with all the usual prayers for the dead. There was the one line that had always stuck with me: *"In the midst of life, we are in death; from whom can we seek help?"* Of course, the answer was supposed to be God. And that was the case, but as I looked at Adam's family and the great number of people in the room it occurred to me another answer was that help came from each other. I knew all too well that to grieve alone was a terrible thing.

Instinctively, I tightened my grip on Adam's hand as it came time for him to give the eulogy. I was glad to be there for him, because I could tell he'd corked his emotions tightly for the day. He proceeded to deliver the perfect off-the-cuff British public statement. It was sincere, but a little humorous, and the kind of speech that would've made his father proud.

After the service, we went back to the house, where Sylvia had seen to it that there was a properly catered event. Adam introduced me to everyone without thinking our guests might recognize me. At first, I thought them all geeky intellectuals and snobby aristocrats who kept themselves at arm's length from the nastiness of American politics. Then an older woman walked straight up to me and held out her hand.

"Hello, I'm Professor Beatrice Hadley. I do believe you're Nicole Johnson."

"Yes, yes, I am." I smiled. "It's nice to meet you, Professor Hadley."

Glancing at Adam, Beatrice said, "I suppose you know Adam from his work at the White House."

"Yes," Adam said. "But actually we knew each other before then."

My eyes darted to his. We hadn't yet discussed what we would tell the world about our past. I thought it best to be completely upfront. "Yes, we're old friends."

Then another professor joined our conversation. Offering me his hand, he said cheerily, "I'm Graham Schofield—I worked with Professor Kincaid. It's nice to meet you, Miss Johnson."

"A pleasure to meet you, Professor Schofield," I said, shaking his hand.

"So, Adam, how is the BBC these days?" he asked, turning to Adam. "Are you still enjoying living in Washington?"

Adam cleared his throat. "Washington is a wonderful city, but actually, I've left the BBC…for the time being."

Both Professors Schofield and Hadley frowned. Obviously, neither understood why he would leave such a plum job. Luckily, his mother had overheard the conversation. She walked over and put her hand on his shoulder. "Adam's decided to take some time off so he can be around if we need his help."

As Mrs. Kincaid swished away, I chimed in, "I'm also looking forward to Adam spending time on his artwork."

He glanced down at me and smiled. "I suppose I'll have time for that."

"Artwork? What would that be?" Professor Hadley was curious.

Adam shrugged. "Oh, political cartoons. It's just a hobby of mine."

"Really? Do you know Richard Lawrence at the *Financial Times?*"

"Only his work. I've never met him. His work is brilliant, though."

"He's a very good friend of mine from school days. We go way back; we were at Stowe together. You know, he's retiring soon. He'll still contribute to the paper, but not daily. If you want, I can introduce you two."

I gave Adam's hand a hard squeeze, and he eagerly answered, "That would be wonderful, Professor Hadley. I'd really appreciate that."

By mid-afternoon, I was dragging. Jetlag had caught up with me, and I couldn't drink enough tea to counteract it. At one point, I closed my eyes as sleep tempted me, and I heard Adam say, "Nicki, let me take you upstairs. You're knackered."

My eyes flew open. "Thank you. I haven't had much sleep."

"I just need to tell Mum."

He bumped into David as he walked away, and I overheard him say, "I'm taking Nicki upstairs for a kip. Can you help out down here if they need me?"

"A kip? Like you're going to let her nap." David smirked.

"Yes, I'm going to let her nap." He leaned into David and muttered quietly, "Do you really think I'm taking her to my room to shag her brains out during my father's wake?"

"Seems like as good a time as any, mate." His smirk widened into a grin. "Everyone's sorted down here."

After talking to his mother and grabbing my bag, Adam led me upstairs to his room. I looked at him skeptically. "Will your mother be okay with this?"

"I'm pretty sure she had cottoned on to the fact we were sleeping together sixteen years ago. I doubt that she'll be upset today." Kissing my forehead, he added, "Besides, with David and his mum here, the house is full. There's no other space. You're stuck with me."

"I like that," I said with a grin.

Walking into his childhood bedroom, I looked around at the walls, which were covered in Liverpool football memorabilia that he'd collected over his lifetime. I laughed. "This is quite a collection."

"I always meant to change it, but never got round to it."

"Oh please. Like you'd really want to take any of this down."

"You're right about that." Smiling at me, he then nodded to the bed. "Bugger, I only just noticed the bed. We might be a little uncomfortable in this small space tonight."

"Never," I murmured, wrapping my arms around his neck. After a long kiss, I smiled. "Don't you remember? We only ever slept together in a twin bed. That's what was in my room in high school."

"Ah! That's right." He touched the hair around my face. "I never wanted to leave."

"I never wanted you to leave." I rose to kiss him again. "And I still don't."

Was it talk of high school? I didn't know, but soon we were making out like the teenagers we used to be. He broke it off just as I felt him get hard. "I should go back downstairs."

"I know. I'm sorry about that." I giggled. "I got carried away."

"Believe me. I want to get carried away with you. I just can't right now."

"Don't let me sleep too long, okay?"

"I won't."

After showing me the "loo" and providing me with a towel, Adam went back to talk to the guests. I changed into a camisole and pajama bottoms and climbed into his bed. Exhausted, I was asleep in minutes.

The next thing I knew, I was having an amazingly sexy dream. Adam and I were making out. I wasn't sure where we were, but his hands were up my shirt. Then he moved them down my pants. It felt so real, I could sense myself getting aroused as he began to touch me just so. As an orgasm began to build, I drifted out of my sleep and realized it wasn't a dream. We weren't making out, but he'd started to touch me when I was sleeping. I smiled but kept my eyes closed. When he hesitated for a second, I mumbled, "Don't stop."

"Then I won't," he said.

I lay there while he touched me in the same way he had so many years ago when we'd messed around. I'd forgotten how good it was to be brought to orgasm with such a simple, steady movement. This time he was a little older and wiser, though, so he played with my breasts simultaneously, pinching and tweaking my nipples so that I felt it everywhere, including my clit below. Arching my back, I clutched the sheets and refrained from my usual orgasmic gibberish. I just mewled and shuddered as I rode it out.

Afterward, I smiled. "That was nice."

"It was nice to watch."

"Was it, now?" I chuckled and reached for his dick and found the evidence. "Well, it appears it was."

"I get off watching you get off." He leaned in for a kiss. "Call me old-fashioned."

"You're old-fashioned, and I like it," I said, pulling him on top of me.

I stripped off his boxers as he kissed me, and then he pulled down my pants. After I kicked them off, he wasted no time and slipped himself inside of me. For a moment, I wondered if we really should be fucking away during his father's wake, but Adam didn't seem to be thinking twice about it. Grief was a crazy experience, and he probably needed the closeness to another person.

Afterward, he caught his breath and kissed my hair, and I looked up at him. "You're smiling."

"I am?" he asked.

"You are."

"Probably because I'm so damn happy."

"Good." I gave him a kiss to punctuate it.

He rolled over and stared at the ceiling. "It's odd, though…feeling this way. I don't think I'm supposed to be cheery after my father has just died. It's very confusing."

"I know. I remember that feeling."

"What do you mean?"

"Way back…when we first started dating. I thought my heart was going to burst. I was so elated…such a giddy teenager. But even though everything felt right between us, I felt like I was doing something wrong—like I'd forgotten about Lauren. Like I should've been in mourning. I couldn't be in mourning, though, not with you around."

"That's exactly how I feel. Maybe if I'd been able to give him a proper goodbye, it would feel differently. Why did he have to go while I was away?"

"Oh, Adam." I ran my fingertips through his hair. "You can't think about it like that. Lauren and I were bickering over something stupid when she died. Why would I want to focus on that? You're not supposed think about the end. The end is full of regret that you can't do anything about." My voice wavered. "You need to remember them living—when they were really alive—not sick or dead in a car."

Tears welled in his eyes. "I think I'd miss him too much if I thought about what he was like before he was ill."

Seeing him cry always touched me, and my own eyes became wet. I stroked his cheek. "You'll always miss him. You just won't miss him all the time, if that makes any sense."

"It does." He smiled.

Kissing his cheek, I whispered, "I love you, Adam."

"I love you." His hand went beneath my chin, and he tipped my face up. "You know, you're making me smile again."

"You make me smile, too." I squeezed him hard. "I'm even happier than I was back then."

"I'm happier as well." And just before he kissed me again, he added, "Because this time we're together for good."

Chapter Nineteen

The next morning, we were packing our bags for the trip to Scotland when Sylvia came in the room with a newspaper in her hand.

"Morning, Nicki. Morning, Adam. I thought you might want to see this."

He grabbed the paper out of her hand. "What's that?"

I peered over his arm as Sylvia answered him, "*The Cambridge News*. Look right here." She pointed to a few photos beside a short story about their father's memorial service. The first photo was a simple shot of the chapel with the crowd of mourners in front of it. The second one showed Adam and his mother greeting some of his father's colleagues. Then there was the third photo. Everyone was quiet.

Eventually, Sylvia said, "It's a darling photo of you two. It would be lovely to frame."

Adam practically snarled at his sister, while I studied the picture. Adam's arms encircled me. His expression was somber, and I was looking off into the distance. *At least we weren't kissing*, I thought. Then I read the caption aloud, "'Cambridge-born BBC White House Correspondent, Viscount Adam Kincaid, consoles himself over the loss of his father with Ms. Nicole Johnson.'"

I sighed, but my profession kicked in at once. "This is going to be picked up somewhere. There are probably other photos, too. Let me call Matt, and you should warn the BBC."

He nodded. "I'll call Kent after you talk to Matt. I need to know what the White House might say."

"I knew you two would want to see this," Sylvia said, "but isn't the bright side that it's a lovely photo?"

"It is a nice one." I smiled, giving into her chipper nature. "Now let me wake up Matt."

I checked the clock. It would be four in the morning DC time. *Great. Matt is going to be pissed.*

"The room next to this is my mum's sewing room. It will be private, and you can ring him from there."

"Thanks," I said.

As I settled into a comfy chair upholstered in chintz and surrounded by a storeroom of sewing and knitting supplies, I took a breath. *How do I break this to Matt?*

When he answered his phone, he sounded alert, probably because he knew if he was getting a call from me at four in the morning, he needed to be on top of things. "Nicole. What's up?"

"Matt, I'm really sorry to bother you, but we have a problem. There was a local photographer at Adam's father's funeral who took a picture of Adam and me hugging. It's in the *Cambridge News* this morning. The tagline identifies me by name."

"Great," he said under his breath. "That's going to get picked up by some shitty British tabloid, and we're going to have to respond."

"I know. That's why I'm calling. What do you want to say?"

After Matt and I worked things out, I found Adam alone at his desk. "How was it?" he asked.

"He wasn't happy, and he won't be for a while, but we came up with a good statement."

"What is it?"

I read from my notes. "If asked, the White House will say that 'Deputy Press Secretary Nicole Johnson was given a few days off to support her old friend Adam Kincaid at his father's funeral. The BBC notified the White House on Tuesday of this past week that Adam Kincaid had resigned.'" I stopped reading and looked up. "That's it. I think it sounds all right. Now go find out what the BBC will say."

"It does work." He smiled. "Just give me a moment to track down Kent."

"Oh, and Matt and I agree it's important that I show up at work on Monday morning. You know — give everything a sense of normalcy."

"That *would* be the best thing. If you stay here, it looks like you're hiding out."

"Unfortunately, that means I'll need to leave tomorrow, after the interment."

"You know, I think David was planning on flying back to the States on Monday. I'm sure he would change his plans to head back with you tomorrow. It might be good to have someone with you in case there are photographers."

"That would be great if he could."

"You know he'd be happy to." He stood up and gave me a quick kiss. "This is going to work out. Now, let me call Kent."

As he walked out of the room, I flopped onto the freshly made bed. Shielding my eyes from the morning sun, I envisioned how awful that Monday morning press briefing would be. I'd be a laughing stock for a while. There was no way out, though, other than to endure it. If I didn't show up, it would be worse and prolong the issue. I just had to suck it up and take it.

A few minutes later, Adam returned with a sardonic smile. "I suppose it's all sort of amusing if you think about it."

"How so?"

"I don't know…" he said as he took a seat beside me on the bed. "In a way, my dad exposed us."

"Of all people."

"Exactly. And listen to this. The *Daily Mirror* called Kent about the photo while he was still speaking with me."

"No. So what did Kent say?"

"He put them on hold while we talked. He asked what the White House response was going to be and said the BBC would make a similar statement." Adam then read aloud from his reporter's notebook. "'Adam Kincaid resigned from the BBC last Monday. We look forward to employing him again if the opportunity arises. The BBC will permanently fill its White House correspondent position shortly. Our condolences go out to Adam and his family as they mourn the loss of the former Viscount Kincaid.'"

"I like how they don't mention me at all."

"I agree. It's better for them as well."

"You don't think the tabloids will try to find us in Scotland?"

"They might, but Kent said when he gets calls from the tabs, he'll advise them it would appear unseemly to stalk us."

"We'll see if they heed his advice," I said with a laugh. I pressed my hands to my cheeks. "Oh, Adam. What a mess."

"We'll get through it," he said, taking me in his arms. "If it means we get to be together, it's more than worth it."

I kissed his cheek. "More than worth it."

As we spent the next few hours traveling by car, plane, and then car again to the Kincaid home in Scotland, the tabloid media was at work. Adam's phone rang so much that he turned it off, and I ignored all calls unless it was Matt.

Sylvia kept looking at us with concern. "Shouldn't you say something?"

"Absolutely not." I shook my head emphatically. "Don't give in to them. No one in the general public will expect him to return a reporter's call when he's burying his father."

"It's true." Adam laughed. "I always knew revealing our relationship would be controversial, but Dad's death is giving it an air of dignity that it wouldn't otherwise receive."

As we drove up the long road to the estate, I felt like I'd either been sent back in time or was on the set of an eighteenth-century costume drama. The ancient-looking buildings were partially covered in vines and set back into a wooded area.

"That's your family house?" I asked.

He looked up briefly from the book he was reading. "That's it. Since the fourteenth century."

Sylvia sniffed the air. "I hate it. Everything smells like wet rock—even in the family quarters, even if it hasn't rained for a month." She looked at the car behind us, which David was driving with Mrs. Kincaid and David's mother. "Poor David. I bet he's having to listen to them gush about it. He hates it, too. He says being here makes him feel like a serf."

"I can see why," I said, gaping at the property. "I'm feeling very inferior myself."

"Ridiculous." Adam gave me a nudge. "It's not like we earned this place or the title. There's no merit involved."

"That's very egalitarian of you, *Viscount* Kincaid." I giggled.

"I won't be using the title, and you know it," he said with another nudge and a kiss.

When we got out of the cars, everyone stretched their legs from the long hours of travel. I admired the idyllic scene of rolling countryside, which seemed to go on for miles. "It's hard to believe that you own this."

"Well, we don't really anymore." He winked. "The nation is kind enough to let us squat."

I looked at the pond off the side of the chapel and then out onto the forest in the distance. "It's a stunning place to squat."

He pulled me to him and whispered in my ear, "Maybe we could live here for a bit. Raise some wee ones with thick Scottish accents that neither of us understand."

My cheeks flamed. Naturally, I'd thought about where things between Adam and me would lead. If we lived together and that worked out, we might get married, and if we got married, we'd definitely have kids. Since he'd mentioned marriage once before, I knew it wasn't a remote thought in his mind. And though it had overwhelmed me the first time, to hear him hint at it again now tickled me to death.

He grinned. "You'd like that wouldn't you? I know I would."

"Do I get to see you in a kilt?" I asked in a deflection.

"Naturally," he said, tousling my hair.

Just as we'd predicted, the tabloids wrote their stories that day. I kept up with Matthew, who confirmed they'd received multiple inquiries about the photograph. He said the White House stuck with its script and ended the calls quickly. The following morning, we checked all the tabloids online. The Cambridge photographer had likely made a mint because he'd sold all the photographs to the *Daily Mirror*—and had evidently captured us doing more than hugging.

David looked over Adam's shoulder at his laptop and whistled. "That's quite a lip-lock you two have in that picture."

"I think it looks sweet," said Sylvia.

"*Sweet?*" David snickered and said beneath his breath, "Maybe sweet in an 'I'm gonna fuck your brains out later' kind of way."

I flashed him a look that said I didn't think it was very funny. "I'm never going to hear the end of it from Matthew."

"If all you're worried about is being made fun of by your boss, I think we're okay," Adam said as he reached for my hand.

"Thankfully, there's not much to their story. It's pretty thin," I said with a nod. "If the coverage continues this way, I think you're right."

After we attended church that morning, the local vicar followed us to the family crypt to inter Professor Kincaid's ashes. As we walked back to the house, Adam said to me, "It's odd that I was more emotional Friday at the memorial service than today."

"Well, that's because he's still alive in a way when we talk about him. There's not much sense of him as a person in a spooky crypt."

We'd been holding hands, then he let go and grabbed my waist. "I wouldn't be getting through this without you."

"Oh yeah, you would."

"No, I wouldn't."

"Well, if that's true, I'm glad to help you because you helped me so much," I said, my voice cracking. "I love you."

He grinned and lifted my chin to kiss me. Just as his lips were about to meet mine, we heard David call from behind, "That'll be the last one of those for a while. I need to get Ms. Johnson to her chariot."

Then he sped past us, but not before hitting Adam's arm. "Don't worry, cuz. I'm a pro at taking care of her."

"Hey!" I laughed. "That was a long time ago."

Adam growled, "You're a dead man."

David didn't even look behind him as he walked ahead. "No worries. I'll safely deposit her, untouched, at my bird's door."

"*Bird?*" I shook my head. "Lisa would not like to know she's been referred to as an animal."

"It really is a term of endearment," Adam said. "I promise."

"Yeah? I can't wait to hear David explain that one to her."

As soon as we landed at Dulles Airport, I called Adam.

"I'm glad to hear you arrived in one piece," he said. "How was the flight?"

"Fine…great, actually. David kindly upgraded me to first class."

"The man who thinks himself a serf…"

"Yes, I have to say that for someone who portrays himself as this guy from the wrong side of the tracks, he certainly enjoys a lavish lifestyle."

"He does. He should be the viscount."

"So what's up? Are there more stories? I haven't called Matt yet."

"Everything else has been regurgitated from the tabloid piece, except for that complete arsehole, Dan Roark. He wrote a few sentences on his blog about us."

"He did not!"

"Yes, he did. It just proves I was right about him all along."

"Why would he do that?"

"Because he's a twat, that's why, and unfortunately, he had a little help from Felicity."

"Oh no." *Hell hath no fury like a woman scorned.* I should've known something like that would happen. "Read it to me, please."

"All right." His proper British accent then changed to a hammed-up American one. It was always funny to hear Adam's interpretation of Americans, and his take on those he hated was the best. He began by clearing his throat. "'There's lots of gossip among the White House Press Corps. I don't know if anything inappropriate happened between Nicole Johnson and Adam Kincaid while he was at the BBC. I do know they used to talk a fair amount while at work. I never saw anything out of the ordinary, but some people said they believed things started between them at the White House Correspondents' Dinner.

"'Then they were seen dancing together rather closely last Saturday night when the president was traveling in Istanbul. It was at a restaurant with many people around, including other members of the press. Kincaid resigned on Monday, and now there are photos of them together. Word on the street is that they knew each other in high school and never got over one another. We'll see what pans out this week.'"

"Asshole," I said bitterly. "How do you know Felicity was involved?"

"The part about never getting over you. She accused me of that when I first started seeing you outside of work."

"I love how he walks a line of not being too accusatory of me. Maybe it's because I did those shots with him."

"Maybe, but I bet it's more that he doesn't want to poison his relationship with the White House in case you stick around."

"His blog is just crap, but unfortunately someone will read it. I'll call Matt to see what he says. Tomorrow is going to suck."

"I know. I'm very sorry about that. Here you thought I was going to be the sacrificial lamb for our relationship, but you're the one who will take the public beating."

"Yes, I will," I said with a gulp. Then I smiled. "But I'll take it if I get to finally be with you."

"That's exactly what I want to hear."

As I shared a Washington Flyer cab back to DC with David, I called Matt. He was still grumbling about the situation. "You've created quite a mess for us to clean up, haven't you?"

"I suppose so. I can't apologize enough." I once again could feel my stomach get queasy with fear. It was only appropriate for me to make my previous offer. "Do you want me to resign? I will."

"No," he said with an added "God no" for emphasis. "I talked it over with Logan. That will just bring more attention to the situation, and, after all, you really didn't compromise the administration."

"Thank you. Thank you for this."

He then laughed. "Not to mention the president pointed out there could be a silver lining in it all."

"What's that?"

"I suggested we use this as a distraction and quietly announce that we're shelving those new banking regulations for now."

"Ah. That makes sense." Presidencies always liked to announce news for which they would surely be attacked when there was a distraction—or on Friday at five in the evening, when most reporters had already filed their stories for the day.

"I thought it was a brilliant idea, if I do say so myself."

"Well, thank you because you're helping me out as well."

"Yes, I am, and don't think I'm going to forget it."

As predicted, the following morning I was the focus of the White House press briefing. The press corps was all over Matt, demanding answers about whether or not the BBC had special access to the White House because of my relationship with Adam. In an effort to cover the BBC's ass, even the rookie reporter joined in the questioning. Matt said no a million different ways and repeated the official statement.

I stood off to the side, staring straight ahead just as I would if the topic had been something entirely different. What else could I do, though? To show emotion would be horrible.

We'd rehearsed that they would offer me the opportunity to speak, so when the time came, Matt turned to me and smiled. "Nicole, would you like to answer any questions?"

"No," I said with a fake smile. "I won't comment on my personal life."

It didn't matter that the White House gave the press little to go on. Somehow, FOX News made its way to Bellaire, Texas. Of all the people they could find there who knew Adam and me, they'd found Meredith Daniels, Adam's old cheerleader girlfriend. I couldn't help the schadenfreude when I saw she hadn't aged well, and she also came across a little bitter.

Staring straight into the TV camera, Meredith declared, "Yes, I knew Adam Kincaid when he lived in Bellaire. We dated for a while. He also dated Nicki Johnson. I don't know what happened with them. I'm surprised she works in the White House. No one ever thought much would come of her."

I called Adam immediately after I saw it. "You will never believe who FOX News dug up to talk about us."

"Who?"

"Your little girlfriend Meredith Daniels."

"You still hate her, even though we're together."

"I'm going to send you the link to the clip. She's a total bitch. Even gets in a dig at me." I summed up my anger: "I bet she's a Republican."

"That's your highest insult." He sniggered.

"Don't laugh. You were with her."

"I thought you forgave me for that."

"I did," I huffed. "I just don't like having it thrown in my face again sixteen years later."

"Nicki, you're the one I'm with now, right?"

"Right." I smiled just at the thought.

"Oh fuck," Adam then said. "That's bloody awful."

"What? What's that?"

"Anderson Cooper is about to interview Dr. Drew about our relationship."

"Ewww. AC, what are you doing to me? Turn it off." I sighed. "I know it's awful, Adam, but we just have to block it out. The story will die eventually."

The story's death came more swiftly than we'd anticipated. The following day, Logan took questions after making some remarks on events in the Middle East.

Dan Roark, the jerk, performed as usual when he asked, "Mr. President, I'm sure you've heard about the relationship between Nicole Johnson and BBC reporter Adam Kincaid. Has your presidency been compromised in any way because of it?"

The president chuckled and shook his head. "Of all the things going on in the world, you ask me about that?"

The room erupted, and Logan waited for the laughter to die down before he continued, "Pardon the joke. But no, of course not. My presidency hasn't been compromised at all by their relationship. Nicole has worked for me since she was in college. She's like a daughter to me and has kept me informed of things. Adam is no longer with the BBC. Nothing has happened to compromise the integrity of any of the parties involved. I don't really see the intrigue — other than it's a nice story."

And that was that. In the public's mind, it was a boring scandal, and if the president announced there was no intrigue, only a love story, then it was so.

Chapter Twenty

While I endured the slings and arrows of the press, Adam was back in England, dealing with his father's estate. He'd been named executor of the will, so there was work to be done there.

Plus, his mother had decided to leave Cambridge and return to London near her sister, David's mom. So there was her move to coordinate as well, but both Sylvia and Adam thought it was the best thing for her to move on with her life, and they liked the fact they'd no longer have to make the trip to Cambridge when they were back in England.

It was two weeks before Adam came back to the States, more than enough time for our scandal to fizzle out. Before he arrived home, I'd worked on a surprise for him for days. Though I was bummed to leave Lisa, my heart was elsewhere, and I wanted to be with him.

If only I could've been a fly on the wall when it came time, but it was one of those surprises that would work best when he was alone. And he wasn't going to be alone for long—or ever again.

Adam Kincaid
Washington, DC
May 2009

After two weeks home with Mum, I left Sylvia to finish with the dispersal of Dad's belongings. I promised to return in a month, but Mum said she was going to Rome with my Aunt Jane. I agreed that a trip out of the country would do her good. Secretly, I was pleased that I could get on with my life. Knowing my mum, that was one of the reasons for her trip.

When I arrived at my flat in DC, I knew I'd have an hour before the dinner date Nicki and I had planned. I went about my usual post-travel routine of divvying up my dirty clothes to take to the cleaners. It was only as I searched for a laundry bag that I noticed there was something different about my bedroom. *The furniture is rearranged.*

I studied the room. Things had been moved around to fit a new dresser off to the side. I smiled and walked straight toward it. Opening the top drawer, I saw a pile of what I recognized as Nicki's knickers. I shut it and pulled the next drawer open. There were her T-shirts, nicely folded. On a hunch, I went into my bathroom. Sure enough, Nicki's toothbrush, hairbrush, and her lotions and potions were stowed in the cabinets and drawers.

When there was a knock at the door, I answered it with a smile. "I don't know why you knocked. You've got a key."

Nicki grinned and ignored my comment as she walked in. After placing her bag down on the ground, she wrapped her arms around me. "I hope you don't mind I made myself at home."

"You are home. With me," I whispered and kissed her forehead.

Closing her eyes, she laid her head on my shoulder. "I am. Finally."

Acknowledgments

The writer's life is supposed to be solitary, but writing this book has been anything but that. Lovely friends have aided me along the way, making it a better, richer story and ensuring that it had commas. Some of these wonderful people include:

My beloved fan fiction community, who a few years ago helped with the beginnings of this book, especially Catherine Waring and Corey Ward.

Azucena Sandoval and Carolina McGoey, who made Juan Carlos the Latin lover that he is.

Daisy Prescott and S.L. Scott, who gave me daily encouragement along with eagle-eye pre-reading.

Elizabeth de Vos, who is a literary scientist in her ability to dissect a manuscript for gaps and inconsistencies.

The wonderful book bloggers out there who urged me on after reading *Beside Your Heart*. You kept Nicki's voice so loud in my head that I had to write the sequel from her point of view.

Omnific Publishing—Elizabeth Harper and Enn Bocci, who put up with me, and most importantly, my editor Colleen Wagner, who is the master of the gentle nudge and saucy British sayings.

I'm forever grateful to all of you and a few more who I would add if I had more space and a better memory. Thank you so very much.

About the Author

Even before she graduated from law school, Mary knew she wasn't cut out to be a real lawyer. Drawn to politics, she's spent her career as an organizer, lobbyist, and non-profit executive. Nothing piques her interest more than a good political scandal or romance, and when she stumbled upon writing, she put the two together. A born Midwesterner, naturalized Texan, and transient resident of Washington, D.C., Mary now lives in Northern California with her two daughters and real lawyer husband.

Singles and Novellas

It's Only Kinky the First Time by Kasi Alexander
Learning the Ropes by Kasi & Reggie Alexander
The Winemaker's Dinner: RSVP by Dr. Ivan Rusilko
The Winemaker's Dinner: No Reservations by Everly Drummond
Big Guns by Jessica McQuinn
Concessions by Robin DeJarnett
Starstruck by Lisa Sanchez
New Flame by BJ Thornton
Shackled by Debra Anastasia
Swim Recruit by Jennifer Lane
Sway by Nicki Elson
Full Speed Ahead by Susan Kaye Quinn
The Second Sunrise by Hannah Downing
The Summer Prince by Carol Oates
Whatever it Takes by Sarah M. Glover
Clarity by Patricia Leever
A Christmas Wish by Autumn Markus
Late Night with Andres by Debra Anastasia

www.ingramcontent.com/pod-product-compliance
Lightning Source LLC
Chambersburg PA
CBHW031949130726
47904CB00012B/861